# About the author

Hiawyn grew up in South Africa, studied English and Drama after school and worked as an advertising copywriter before becoming a full-time writer. Since then, she's had over ninety children's books published all over the world including picture books, poetry, plays, young fiction, story collections and the scripts and lyrics for two musicals, *The Vackees* and *The Mermaid*. Her work in children's television includes development and scripts for the animated series *Sheeep*, *Marvellous Milly*, *Wilf the Witch's Dog* and *Big Cat, Little Cat*. The animated series *Mona the Vampire* is based on her books with Sonia Holleyman. Most recently, Hiawyn has written the *Rumblewick* series for Orchard, about a cat and his unwilling witch.

ORCHARD BOOKS
338 Euston Road, London NW1 3BH
*Orchard Books Australia*
Level 17/207 Kent Street, Sydney, NSW 2000

ISBN 978 1 84616 336 4

First published in 2008 by Orchard Books
A paperback original
Text © Hiawyn Oram 2008
A CIP catalogue record for this book is
available from the British Library.

1 3 5 7 9 10 8 6 4 2

Printed in Great Britain
Orchard Books is a division of Hachette Children's Books,
an Hachette Livre UK company.
www.orchardbooks.co.uk

# BEING
# IMPOSSIBLE

## HIAWYN ORAM

ORCHARD BOOKS

To Katie S. with thanks

# Chapter 1
# Now

I like to watch dominoes falling. My boyfriend sets them up on the table in his room at college.

He has a knack for setting up dominoes. A whole box of them in a long curvy line. When he says 'ready', I flick the first one with my fingernail. And down they go in a slow, sure ripple. Clack, clack, clack. Each helpless not to follow the domino before. I like the fact that the last tile ends up flat on its back only because the first one fell.

This chain of dominoes falling. It reminds me of the way things happen that make other things happen which, in turn, change all things for ever in ways they wouldn't have changed if the original thing hadn't occurred in the first place.

In the chain of events that altered me and my

family for all time, you could say the first domino to topple was my grandfather.

He tripped over a cracked paving stone in Melbourne, Australia and broke his hip.

This made my mother catch the first plane out to take care of him, which brought a strange thin woman to take care of us.

Her name was Eve Everett and with her came a bird – a child-hating parrot called Mimi.

Almost the moment they moved in my father put his DO NOT DISTURB sign on his study door and my older sister Verity went to stay with her best friend, Farah.

If these things hadn't happened I wouldn't have been sulking in the vegetable garden when I was. If I hadn't been in the vegetable garden when I was, I wouldn't have found Tiff. If Tiff hadn't come into our household, I can't imagine how my life would be. Probably still impossible.

But, luckily these things did take place and this is that story…hard to believe for some but perfectly true anyway.

# Chapter 2
# BONYFINGERS
# MOVES IN

At the airport our mother hugged us in turn. 'Now, take care of your dad and each other and be nice to Mrs Everett. Once you get to know her you'll see…she's a lovely person.'

Verity mocked. 'Mum! She's a skeleton who wears too much jewellery and her hair is practically mauve!'

Our mother glanced at our father for support. (Though she needn't have bothered. He was gazing into the distance, not listening as usual.) 'I've known Eve Everett since I was eighteen,' she said. 'She taught me at Nursing College and she's a dear. Now please…for Grandad's sake, all pull together.'

There was nothing to do except nod and hide our tears and let her do what she needed to do – get to her broken father.

There was nothing to do about Mrs Everett either because when we got back from the airport, there she was. Already moving in.

Her rust-coloured car was parked in the drive. Her suitcases and a TV were piled in the hall and she was fussing over a scruffy parrot in a white metal cage.

'This is Mimi!' she announced. 'And Mimi…' she jangled her bracelets and pointed a bony finger at each of us, 'this is Mr Dempster, Paul, Verity, little George and…uh…Logan, as in the loganberry, I assume,' (meaning me).

Mimi made a rude noise. Mrs E ignored it. 'Mimi will live with me in my room since she does so *hate children.*'

*Hate children!* The parrot mimicked her, its eyes darting.

'Well, that's not a very suitable pet for someone who takes *care* of children.' Dad looked shaken. 'Did my wife agree to this?'

Mrs Everett frowned, then remembered who was boss and gushed, 'Of course, Mr Dempster, your wife knows all about Mimi! Now, Paul and George, please take my cases up to my room. I'll need the afternoon to settle in.'

'Sure,' said Paul, easy-going as always. 'I'll take the

big ones, you take the little ones, George.'

'OK,' George mumbled. He stepped up to Mimi's cage.

'Why *does* she hate children, Mrs Everett? Maybe she doesn't really know any…'

He was about to put his finger through the bars to stroke Mimi. Mrs Everett rapped his hand. '*Never* do that, young man! Unless you want to lose a finger!'

George gasped. A bright red patch appeared on each of his cheeks.

Mrs E blushed herself, then lifted Mimi's cage and set off up the stairs. The cage was difficult to manage. Paul politely offered to help. She refused.

'OK,' he said, cheerfully, 'let's get these cases done, George, then we'll go out with our boards.'

The boys struggled with the luggage. Verity and I pleaded silently with Dad. *Do not leave us alone to cope with this woman and her hate-filled parrot.*

He did not meet our eyes – just rubbed his forehead and disappeared into his study with an embarrassed 'Hmmmph'.

# Chapter 3
# MY FATHER AND MY SLOT THEORY

I don't like saying it but I have to: my father has never been a normal father. In fact, come to think about it, he has never been normal, full stop.

For a start, he is a composer. At this time, while the first dominoes in this story were falling, he composed nothing but weird experimental music with more silences in it than notes.

When he was composing, he always hung a 'DO NOT DISTURB' sign on his study door. And, as he was almost always composing, 'DO NOT DISTURB' was almost always on his door.

Once, when no one else was home and I cut myself, I had to interrupt him. He stared without seeing me. Only when some of the blood dripped onto one of his precious noteless scores, did he pull himself together and try to help.

Of course, we knew he loved us. Some days you could feel it coming off him like radar beams. Sometimes he'd sit at the kitchen table listening to us as if talk had just been invented and we were its inventors. In those moments he seemed to glow with the excitement of having us for his own.

Otherwise, he never took or fetched us from school like the other fathers who worked at home. He never helped us with our mother's birthday. He never came on holiday with us and he never played any kind of ball game with Paul and George.

Our mother said it was because he was a genius and we should not expect him to be any other way. I accepted that – because of my theory.

I call it the Theory of Slots and this is how it goes: in every family there are just so many Slots (or roles, as in chances to be something).

Once someone in a family has taken a Slot – e.g. the Rebel Slot or the Maths Boff Slot or the Ace Footballer Slot or whatever – that's it. No one else can occupy it because there's only room for one person at one time in each Slot.

Other members of the family have to circle round until they find an empty Slot they want and then – if they've got their wits about them – quickly pounce and grab it.

People prove the theory all the time without even knowing it: *Oh, she's the clever one in the family,* they say. *He's the sporty one. She's the creative one, you know.*

Luckily, because kids are always changing, they don't have to stay in the same Slot forever. With grown-ups, it's the opposite. They can choose how they're going to be before any of their children are born. That's how they get the Slots they really want. And once a grown-up is in one, mostly there's no getting them out of it. They're there for life.

And so it was with our father. He'd bagged the 'I-Am-A-Genius-So-I-Am-Excused-If-I'm-Weird' Slot before any of us came along. Now, if one of us wanted to be The Mad Loner doing something only forty-nine people in the world are interested in, we couldn't be. He was there. He had that role and he wasn't budging.

Anyway, back to the day Mrs Everett and her parrot moved in. Having disappeared into his study, Dad reappeared. He placed his DO NOT DISTURB sign on its hook – crooked, because he wasn't watching what he was doing – and closed the door in the way he always did – *tight, shut, keep out.*

A moment later we heard the high soft notes of his glockenspiel.

'OK.' Verity pouted her pretty mouth. 'I can see what's going to happen. He'll be in there night and day and we'll have to cope with Mrs Bonyfingers by ourselves. It's so unfair. Hey, d'you know what I'm going to do?'

I shook my head though I had a fairly good idea: she was going to ask her best friend Farah if she could go and stay at her house.

And I was right.

She tossed her long blonde hair. 'I know her mum'll say yes. She adores me.'

Out came her pink and silver mobile. Gliding on perfect willow-wand legs, she slid into the sitting room and lay on the sofa – all the time chattering excitedly to Fa.

Watching her now – lolling about, gracefully occupying the 'I'm–So–Pretty–And–Adorable–I–Don't–Have–To–Do–Anything' Slot – I could see she was going to slide out of this situation. And it made me spit.

If Verity went to Farah's and Dad withdrew completely, what would I have to become in our motherless household? The One Pretending Everything Is All Right When It Isn't? The One Having To Pair

Socks With Bonyfingers? The One Having To Cover Up For Our Father's Weirdness?

Well, I wasn't going to do it. I wasn't.

And there was another thing that was upsetting me. It was that *way* she talked to Farah, as in, *we have a secret world, keep out.*

It reminded me of how I didn't have anyone to talk with like that. Not now, because, while I'd been home from school with a bug (attacking everything from my throat to my stomach), my best friend, Cammy, had become huggermugger mates with Clarissa Clarke!

Now *they'd* become the inseparable ones – even texting each other when sitting on the same bus!

All I could do was hang about at their edges like a discarded moon from a newly important planet, hoping one of them might remember *I'd like a text too.*

It was clear my life was going dung-ball shaped.

If I wasn't careful I could soon be in the 'Dung-Beetle' Slot – trying to stop my dung-ball life from rolling back and crushing me.

So what was I going to do about it?

The usual: go outside to my secret thinking place to consider.

# Chapter 4
## *I CHOOSE IMPOSSIBLE

The old aviary was this secret place, set in a recess in the wall of the vegetable garden.

Once, when my father decided to study birdsong for something he was composing, it had been wired over and filled with finches and warblers and wagtails.

The wire and the birds were long gone. I'd dragged an old bench into the space and could sit cross-legged there, back against the brick – well-hidden from any view from any window of the house.

So far no one knew this was where I came to sulk. Or when I had important things to decide.

Now, sitting hunched up, staring at the spidery neglected vegetables no one seemed to pick or eat,

I soon heard Paul and George clattering off down the street on their skateboards, talking about ollying and kickflips.

It struck me that neither of them were that put out by the presence of Bonyfingers and parrot in our house or the absence of our mother – or the weirdness of Dad.

Maybe it was me making too much of it. *Be like them,* I tried telling myself. *Take this in your stride!*

But how could I be like Paul? He had the 'Lopey-Good-At-Everything' Slot. No wonder he was always in such a good mood, so cool and laid-back. He'd got 'The King' Slot. Every girl in his school thought he was crush material.

And I couldn't be like George either. He'd slipped right into the 'Always-Brimming-With-Joy' Slot soon after he was born. He was six now and seemed to have no plans to move out of it. He was what he wanted to be without thinking about it, without hurting a fly.

As for me, I'd tried quite a few different roles in my twelve years. When I was eight, I'd occupied the 'One-Day-I'll-Be-Famous-You'll-See' Slot. Then, when no one took that very seriously, the 'No-One-Understands-Me-But-God' Slot. Recently I'd been the family Drama Queen, turning every tiny event into a mega-production. But to be a good Drama Queen, you need to have a willing audience. My mother had been that audience. Now she was halfway to Australia.

I sat on, as the afternoon turned into evening, picking absent-mindedly at the fronds of moss growing on the bench. Doing my best not to face up to the fact that even if I hadn't found the right Slot for myself, everyone else probably thought I was already in it!

'Oh, that Logan,' I could hear them saying, 'she's *The Odd One* of the Dempster children.'

Then – as night fell – I became aware of *something else*. A presence. Something in the dark garden that hadn't been there before.

Eyes were watching me from under the mulberry tree. They were wide, yellow eyes. Attached to nothing. Belonging to nobody. I tried not to blink in case they disappeared.

But no one can not move their eyelids for ever.

I blinked and they vanished.

Even so, it seemed that just from being there at all, the eyes had jolted me out of my slump and beamed the clear white light of a thought into my head. It was this: *there WAS a Slot for me in the*

21

*circumstances — empty, free, and mine to take if I wanted it.*
*And I did want it.*

I'd step right into it now…and strike back.

I would become…*impossible.*

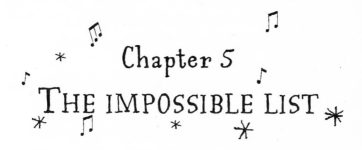

# Chapter 5
# THE IMPOSSIBLE LIST

It isn't easy being impossible if it doesn't come naturally. I didn't know this yet and rushed upstairs to my room to make a list of 10 THINGS TO DO TO BE IMPOSSIBLE.

Later I crossed out the 10 and replaced it with 15 because I thought of 15 things. This was the final list:

1) When someone speaks to you, only answer with a grunt or sneer. Or go completely silent. Silence is a smart weapon.

2) Do the opposite of what you're told to do.

3) Do dangerous things that make them WORRY about you. (Question. What?)

4) Make your room a serious tip. NEVER tidy it even if grounded for refusing.

5) When grounded, go out anyway. (Problem. Where to?)

6) Run away a lot. (Problem again. Where to??)

7) Learn how to graffiti or something similar. (Graffiti dustbins, wall at end of garden, letter boxes, back of bus-stop seats and shelters, walls in bedroom.)

8) Be v. rude to Mrs E because she's what Mum would call a guest in the house.

9) Don't come straight home after school at least three times a week.

10) Play music v. loud.

11) Pretend you've got a boyfriend and are kissing him and it could be leading to other things.

12) Disturb Dad. (??? Bang on his door then run.)

13) Never do homework.

14) Get expelled. (How? Never doing homework may help.)

15) Shoplift and get caught on purpose. Then do it again.

I stuck the list on my wall with Blu-tack so I could put a tick against each item when I'd achieved it. I started with No 4.

Unlike anyone else I knew of my age, I hated mess. But now I pulled half my clothes from their hangers and threw them on the floor. I strung jewellery across my dressing table. Hurled shoes into the air. Let them fall where they fell.

I scooped everything off the bedside table and spread it around. By kicking it.

I emptied the wastepaper bin near the bed and did the same to its contents.

Then I unmade the bed and surveyed my work.

Hate it or not, it was a tip well made.

You could hardly tell it was artificial.

I took a fat felt pen and made a big red tick against No 4 on The List.

Then, to stop me thinking about the mess I was in, I took the cover off my model theatre.

This theatre, which I'd been lovingly building for months, was, I suppose, equivalent to a young kid's happy rag.

It was where I turned when I needed soothing or – in this case – when my life was going dungball shaped.

The base of the theatre was a box – open front and back – made from pieces of 15 mm plywood. To this day I remember the measurements – 60 cm wide by 40 cm deep – carefully glued and tacked together, painted midnight blue and stencilled on the sides with gold columns.

I'd constructed two fluted pillars by folding card into fine pleats, painting them gold too and gluing them to the sides of the stage area.

There were red velvet front-of-stage curtains – made from a remnant Mum had found at the Burton market. And now I was creating 'the wings' (where in a real theatre actors waited to go on stage) out of one of Mum's finished-with black nylon slips – cutting it into pieces which, once hemmed, I planned to hang across each side of the theatre on net-curtain wire.

Attached to a piece of dowelling rod, across the roof of the stage, were six cardboard 'spotlights' constructed from matchboxes and painted black.

About these spotlights, I had a dream.

I wanted them to work – at the flick of a switch. And I was planning, when the moment was right, *to ask Gerald* to make them do so.

Gerald was in our class. He was an electronics wizard. The Boy Genius. According to our teacher he was a great scientist in the making. He could explain anything – even the difference between analogue and digital television if you could be bothered to listen.

He was also the coolest boy in our class, probably in the whole school. Mostly – or this was my theory – because he wasn't concerned with what anyone thought of him.

This set him apart and made him free.

It also made him difficult to get near.

I'd sat two desks away from him all term, but if you'd asked him about me I'm sure he'd have said, '*Who?*'

Still, I figured, until I'd actually approached him about switching on the lights and he'd said no, there was no reason not to dream.

I was doing exactly that when Verity flounced in without knocking.

She looked at the state of my room in horror.

'Hey, this is not like you. What's happened? Bomb explode or something? Anyway, The Bony One says to tell you supper's ready.'

'OK!' I said cheerfully, forgetting to sneer or grunt as per No 1 on The Impossible List.

As soon as she'd gone, I remembered and realised with a thrill. This first supper with Bonyfingers was the perfect place to start showing what I now was...*Logan, The Impossible One.*

# Chapter Six
# THE FIRST SUPPER

Dad was having salad on a tray in his study (surprise, surprise).

There were just us kids and Mrs Everett in the kitchen. She'd heated a cottage pie that Mum had left and overcooked some Brussels sprouts.

I scowled as the others slammed into their chairs with their usual clattering.

Verity was texting at speed on her phone.

Paul and George were analysing their afternoon's skateboarding.

'Thank you! Can we all calm down!' Bonyfingers ordered. 'Verity, turn off that phone, please. We don't communicate with people not present at meals, do we, dear? And you, young George, not so excitable.'

She banged the pie and sprouts down on the table. Verity pretended to switch off.

Bonyfingers said in a holy voice, '*Now who will say grace?*'

We kids exchanged surprised looks. (Ours was not a religious family – at all.)

'Logie will,' said Paul. 'She's the only one of us who's ever been close to God.'

Mrs E sounded genuinely sad. 'I'm sorry to hear that. But very well. Logan, if you will.'

Great, I thought. The perfect opportunity for The Smart Weapon. I curled my lip back and examined the back of my spoon – in silence.

So Paul, being perfect, stepped in. 'Don't worry, Mrs Everett. I'll say it.' He paused. 'In Latin.'

He bowed his head and in a low, bishopy voice said, '*Epirorum appella morgum gratia deus. Amen.*'

There were stifled giggles from Vee and George, who knew he didn't know one word of Latin.

Bonyfingers raised her eyebrows. She wasn't sure if Paul was making fun of her or if his grace was real.

What could she do? She chose, 'Very nice, Paul,' and began to eat.

'Bon appetit,' said Verity, pronouncing the end of the word as 'tit' on purpose. Winking at Paul, she began to work out single bits of mince from the pile on her plate. 'Do you speak any languages, Mrs Everett?'

Bonyfingers looked embarrassed. 'I haven't had the time or the opportunity to learn.'

'I'll teach you what French I know while you're here, if you like,' said Verity. 'And, of course, Paul can teach you Latin.'

Mrs Everett's lip quivered as the others stifled more giggles. It crossed my mind how miserable it must be for her. Coming into our ramshackle house with us kids ranged against her and our father behind his sternly shut door, nowhere near to help.

But to Be Impossible, you cannot allow yourself a single forgiving thought. I pushed mine away.

The others babbled on, talking about nothing. And from me? Not a single word. Not even a grunt.

Eventually Bonyfingers noticed. 'You're very quiet, Logan. Are you always like this?' she said as she banged down a nasty-looking pudding.

I shrugged and examined my spoon again.

'Well?' She appealed to the others. 'Is she always like this? Or has the cat got her tongue?'

'Actually,' said George seriously, 'we don't have a cat so it couldn't have got her tongue. Usually Logan talks all the time…well, I mean when…'

He lost the thread of what he was saying under

Bonyfingers' stare and stuck his bowl forward to change the subject. 'That looks good. I'll have some, if you like.'

Bonyfingers filled George's bowl. 'We all have to learn to toss the ball of conversation at table, Logan. Now, let us begin. Did you have a nice afternoon?'

I wanted to say: *What do you think…my mother's halfway round the world. My father's shut in his study. My sister's abandoning us for her best friend. I don't even have a best friend any more, and you've moved in with a hate-filled parrot.*

But that would have been speaking when I was spoken to. Completely against No 1 on The Impossible List.

So I growled, 'Nah ver.'

'Sorry?' said Bony. '*Nah ver?* What does that mean?'

'When Logie's in a mood,' said Paul, 'it's best to leave her alone. That's what we do.'

'But not what I do,' said Bony, using one of her bony fingers to rattle her necklaces. 'You and I will sit here, Logan, and have a conversation. So what did you do on this "*Nah ver*" afternoon?'

As if she'd organised it, Verity's phone bleeped.

'Oh, sorry, I thought I'd turned it off. But it's only a text. Can I read it? Oh, I have already. It's from Farah…yes! Her mum says I can go and stay.

Coo…ul! Oh, but what'll I take? Logie, you'll have to help me pack. You'll have to!'

She jumped up, grabbed my arm and propelled me towards the door. 'You do understand, Mrs Everett,' she fluttered her long lashes, which should have been pale and blonde (like her hair) but weren't; they were naturally beautifully strangely *dark*. 'Logie can't sit here. I need her upstairs!'

I let myself be rushed away as Bonyfingers called, 'Logan, we have not finished our conversation. So you will come back at once or I'll have to speak to your father!'

At the door, I turned and snarled, '*JUS-TRY!*'

# Chapter 7
## MY CAT COMES TO ME

As Verity pushed me upstairs, she didn't draw breath. 'Fa's mum said they'll come for me in an hour. How can I pack in an hour? And I suppose I'll have to tell Dad. Or would you? Please, Logie. Just tell him Mum arranged it. He won't know the difference.'

On the landing, she was surprised I went towards my room and not hers.

'Logie! You said you'd help me pack!'

Typical: she'd ordered me to help her pack but now it was me who'd promised I would.

And on she went in her adorable way.

'I mean I got you out of there, didn't I? If it wasn't for me you'd be sitting there all night tossing the ball of conversation with *that woman*. By the way, did I tell you? Fa's got a cousin. *And* he's got a crush on me just from seeing a photograph!'

Laughing, she went into her room. I went to mine. I took the fat felt pen and made a red tick beside No 1 (sneering, grunting and silence) and No 8 (rude to Mrs E) on The List.

I put 'Winds of Change' by Storm into an old CD player Paul gave me when he got his new one and turned it up to the highest volume. Good. Drown the house in noise as per No 10 on The List. Another fat tick.

The music was so loud that when the voice-message alert rang on my phone I nearly didn't hear it.

It was from Cammy. She must have phoned while I was downstairs. *Hi, Logie!* came her longed-for voice. *I know I said you could come over to mine tomorrow but Clarky's asked me to go skating at that new rink in Letford Mall. Anyway, got to go but call or text. Bye.*

My insides twisted. Before the Bug Attack, Cammy wouldn't have wanted to go skating with Clarky or anyone else unless I was there too. Now she didn't seem to think of saying those crucial words...*why don't you come with us?*

At that point, Verity banged on the door and yelled, 'Turn that racket down,' then made a racket herself getting a suitcase out of the landing cupboard and

36

singing at the top of her voice.

I did turn down the music because I couldn't hear myself think. And then, after a bit, in the quiet, my phone rang.

I answered in case it was Cammy again.

It wasn't. It was Verity. 'Logie, listen, something so terrible's happened you have to help. I'm in the bathroom. Please come right now or I may die!'

She wasn't exaggerating. To my mind, the 'so terrible' thing was so awful, if it had been me I *would* have died. (And when it did happen to me, which apparently it was going to any time soon, I probably would die.)

Verity had got her period. She'd been having them for over a year now. Each time she professed to hate it as much as the first, when she'd sobbed, 'If I have to go through *this* every month for the rest of my life, I wish I'd been born a boy.'

When I got to the bathroom she was moaning, 'Why? Why? Why now when Mum's not here and I'm going to Fa's and her cousin fancies me and I haven't got anything? Logie, you'll have to go and look in Mum's bathroom. She always has supplies. Only don't bring those big night-time ones because I won't use them ever in my whole life whatever happens.'

Another great chance to be impossible. I snarled,
'*Whyshdi?*'

'Logie!' she pleaded. 'What's got into you? Think of
someone besides yourself. Help me!'

OK, I thought. Maybe a sister needing sanitary
towels is an exception to the Being Impossible rules.

So I went on the hunt for her.

The cupboard in Mum and Dad's bathroom was
musty and full of toothpaste, rolls of loo paper and old
half-used remedies. It seemed Mum had been too busy
going to Australia in an emergency to leave 'period
supplies'. I rummaged round and eventually found,
crushed at the back of a shelf, a rumpled packet.
Almost empty but not quite. Exactly the wrong kind,
of course, but better than nothing.

Going back through the bedroom I nearly slammed
into Dad.

'Logie! What…' He kept his eyes off what I was
holding. 'Looking for toothpaste?'

Normally, I'd have nodded and let him off
the hook.

But not now. Not now I was impossible.

I sneered, 'No, not toothpaste. Period stuff, Dad,
because that's what girls have in case you won't admit
it. *PERIODS!*'

He was stunned by my outburst, I could see.

When had I ever been rude to him before? Never.

He stammered, 'Uh…OK…uh see you later…oh and…tell Verity her friend's mother called to check if she can go and stay with them. I said she could …that's if…well…if..'

He escaped into their bathroom. I wanted to bang on the door and scream '*If what?*'

Why couldn't he finish the sentence the way I'm sure he meant to? Why couldn't he have said… 'If that's all right with you, Logie, and the rest of you?' Then I could have answered truthfully, '*No, it's not all right. I need my sister here!*'

But, as always with our father, everything was left in the air – in the silences between the notes.

I went back to Vee with the sanitary towels – the night-time kind she'd never ever use in her whole life.

'Oh well…they'll just have to do.' She cheered up as only she can, in the non-space between one second and another. 'Farah'll have some OK ones and if she doesn't her mum'll take us to the 24/7 garage shop.'

She didn't even thank me for coming to her rescue. It was as if, period organised, she'd forgotten I existed.

I tried to hate her but when Farah and her mother came to collect her I was plunged into misery at her going.

We all (except Mrs E) stood in the drive, waving

goodbye – me trying to keep a sneer on my face while tears pricked behind my eyes.

Perfect Paul challenged George to a race back to the sofa and let him win.

I figured no matter how many lights were on, the house was too dark to be in. Anyway, I wanted to see if the yellow eyes under the mulberry tree were a figment of my imagination or attached to something.

I took my MP3 player, a torch and a rug and slipped out unseen to the aviary.

With a bit of luck, I thought, I'd eventually be missed and they'd start to get concerned. (No 3 on The List: make them worry about you.) Then, I could deliberately not answer when they started calling for me and they'd think I'd run away. Better and better. For that I could give No 6 on The List at least half a big fat red tick.

As 'Don't Walk Away' by The Galaxy Girls pounded in my ears, I flashed the torch round the vegetable garden to the mulberry tree pouring out its branches like a huge black fountain.

And there they were. The two yellow jewels. The eyes.

Now, in the torchlight, I could see they belonged not to nobody – but to a big black cat.

We sat summing each other up.

Then, slowly the cat stood, first on all fours, then on her back legs. Without taking her eyes off me, she placed a front leg on a branch and leaned like a human being might lean, swaying slightly.

I thought, any minute now she's going to walk over – upright – like a cat in a cartoon.

She dropped back onto all fours and disappeared into the undergrowth. I snapped off the torch and waited, breath held, not moving a muscle.

The next thing, she was crouching in front of the bench.

She rubbed against a leg of the bench, stretched, flashed her yellow eyes and…PADOOF…jumped into my lap.

Huge and blacker than the night itself, my cat had come to me.

# Chapter 8
## BONYFINGERS HAS A FIT

In my lap, she immediately started purring in mega-decibels.

'Are you lost or have you come to stay?' I whispered against her neck, noticing there was no collar.

She didn't move or look at me, just kept on purring.

I continued: *Listen, cat, and listen carefully. Brush your nose with a paw if you're lost and you'd like to find your way home. But if you've come here to be mine then make a sign…make a noise, any noise.*

She made no sign, just purred.

*Come on. Answer me. I have to know.*

Still only the purring.

I struggled down from the bench with her in my arms.

'All right,' I said. 'I'm going to take you inside and give you something to eat. But if you aren't here for me, then don't get my hopes up. Jump out of my arms this minute and go back to where you came from.'

Now she did stir but not to jump away. She looked up at me and winked – both yellow eyes at once – and settled deeper into my arms.

And that was that as far as I was concerned. I'd done all I could to make sure she was meant to be mine.

Leaving rug, torch and MP3 on the bench, I staggered inside with my bundle.

George was in the kitchen and he flipped. 'Oh he's beautiful. Can we keep him? Can he sleep in my room? Can I feed him? Please, let me. Wow. His purring's like a motorbike!'

'She's a she, George, not a he,' I said.

How did I know this? I just did. I had from the moment I saw her.

Perfect Paul came in and gave her a stroke but he wasn't that interested. He saw her as a distraction for George. So far he'd been amusing George non-stop so he wouldn't miss Mum. Now he took his chance to hand him over to me and get on with his own evening.

'What about a name, and what about feeding

him…her?' George screeched with excitement, already raiding cupboards for tins of fish. 'There's tuna and sardines, look! What about Tunakins for a name?'

'TUNAKINS, George?!' I yelped, completely forgetting to snarl or sneer. 'Would you like to be called TUNAKINS?'

This sent us both into hysterics.

'Anyway,' I said proudly when we pulled ourselves together. 'Her name is…Tiff.'

It came out of my mouth as if someone had put it there.

'Tiff?' George was disappointed. 'Then how about more than one name. How about Tiff Tunakins?'

This sent us back into hysterics, which brought Bonyfingers into the kitchen, rattling like a jewelled skeleton.

She took one look at Tiff and screamed, 'And what is *that* doing in here?'

Tiff withdrew under the kitchen table.

'Get it out!' Bonyfingers yelled. 'I only took this job because your mother assured me there were no pets in the house. And a cat, well…this has gone too far. Now I really will have to speak to your father.'

Jangling furiously, she made for Dad's study.

George called after her in his joyous way, 'Watch

45

out for his DO NOT DISTURB sign, Mrs Everett! If it's up you can't go in.'

Bonyfingers frothed as she stormed off. 'We'll soon see about that!'

George and I followed her, me carrying Tiff.

Dad's sign was up, of course. Bonyfingers didn't care. She banged her fist on the door. (I thought of the times I'd wanted to do that.)

Almost at once the telephone on the hall table rang. George pounced on it. He and I knew it would be Dad wanting to know who had dared knock. (Was there any family in the world like ours – who phoned each other from different rooms in the *same house*? *And* we all had our own phones – except George – even though Mum was always saying we had no money. But that's how weird we were.)

George gabbled sweetly into the receiver, 'Sorry, Dad. It was Mrs Everett knocking. See, Logie's found a cat called Tiff. Though I want her name to be Tunakins. She's beautiful, Dad, and she wants to stay with us, you can tell. Only Mrs Everett says we can't keep her…'

Bonyfingers snatched the phone. 'Mr Dempster! Your wife specifically told me there would not be so much as a pet's hair in this house. Yet now there's a huge black cat in your daughter's arms. Will you

46

come and do something about it?'

Dad's door opened. He seemed calm. He looked us all over – me holding the enormous purring Tiff.

When he eventually spoke, his voice was crumpled. 'Is it on account of your…uh…parrot that you're …concerned, Mrs Everett?'

'Of course, I told you…'

'Fine,' Dad interrupted. 'Tomorrow we'll sort something out. Tonight, Logan, you keep the cat shut in…uh…your room, I suppose…and Mrs Everett… uh…you keep your parrot in yours. Neither need meet the other. Now excuse me, I'm in the…middle of something. Good night.'

He slipped back into his study.

Mrs E swept past, throwing us a furious look, and jangled her way upstairs. We heard her bedroom door close and her high voice talking silly nothings to Mimi.

George and I grinned at each other. We had the same feeling: grown-ups being what they are, if we were allowed to keep Tiff for one night, there was a chance they'd change their minds, *give in* – and we'd be allowed to keep her, full stop.

On that, we couldn't have been more wrong.

# Chapter 9

## ALIEN, MUTANT OR MIRACLE, TIFF TALKS TO ME

In the meantime, for that one night, we fell asleep together – my cat and me. Me, under the bedclothes. She on top, snuggled against my tummy.

I set the alarm on my mobile for 6.30 am the next morning so I could take her out for a wee before she piddled on my carpet.

As soon as the alarm went, I was wide awake, remembering with a rush of happiness I now had a cat. It took me a moment to realise that, if this was true, she was no longer with me on the bed.

I groped for the bedside-light switch. As I groped, I was aware, in the early greyness, that the lamp on my dressing table was already on.

Then I saw her.

And mega-shock wasn't even in it.

She was sitting at my dressing table, where all my jewellery was still spread from me making the mess – *sitting upright like a person* – in a pool of light from the lamp. Her head was on one side, her pink tongue curling up towards her nose.

There was no question about it. She was trying to decide which piece of jewellery to try on. After a bit she picked up – yes, picked up – as if her paws were as easy to use as hands – a gold chain with a coral-coloured droplet.

She held it up against the black fur at her throat. I can't imagine what my face looked like. A fish out of water, gasping?

And then it got scarier.

She turned on the seat, so gracefully, she might as well have been a film star and said…yes, *said*…in a deep, throaty, almost-American accent, 'Do you like it on me?'

OK, I know it's hard to believe. But I'm not inventing it. A cat, sitting upright, trying on a necklace, had spoken to me in words I could perfectly understand. And it didn't stop there.

'Well, do you?' She put the chain down, rummaged around and picked up a necklace I'd got from a stall at the Burton Saturday market. 'Or this one?' She held it up to her neck. 'I like

50

the turquoise in this. Very lucky, you know.'

I was now terrified…a huge, black cat was talking to me in my room! Maybe she was an alien or some kind of mutant. Maybe, if she could sit up like a person and talk in a film-star accent, she could turn on me…like that gross fly-mutant in that gross film…and attack me…eat me, even.

I lay, rigid, turning my eyes back to the table without moving my head.

She climbed off the chair and padded over to the bed. There she put her front paws up beside me and purred, looking like a normal cat.

But, normal cat she was not.

Fixing me with her yellow eyes, she put a paw onto my frozen arm and stroked it.

'You mustn't be afraid,' she said in her throaty, film-star voice. 'I can't help it if you can understand what I say. I can't help what I am – a most unusual cat with talents that far exceed those of any other member of my species. Now, come on, Logan, get over the shock. I'm here to help, not hurt. So how about you get dressed and we go for a walk? It's a fresh day out there. And besides, I need to relieve myself and it's getting urgent.'

She dropped back onto the floor, padded over to the door and sniffed along the gap at the bottom.

I hurried to dress while she arranged herself – again like any normal cat – and started her morning wash.

As I pulled on some clothes, all of me shaking, I lectured myself to keep calm: *Tiff is a talking cat and she's come to you. Not someone else. You. So if she's a mutant or an alien, who cares…a talking cat is just so cool, it's ice!*

'Come on!' I whispered when I was ready. 'We must go as quietly as we can, so as not to wake anyone…especially *her*.' (Meaning Bonyfingers.)

She bounded down the stairs – not quietly at all – PADOOF, PADOOF – while I tiptoed behind.

I unlocked the back door and we stepped together into the new day.

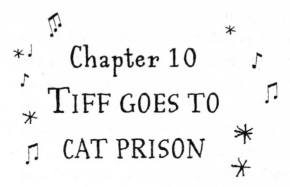

# Chapter 10
# TIFF GOES TO CAT PRISON

Out in our overgrown garden, Tiff shot off over the long dew-soaked grass to do her piddling in the bushes in private.

She seemed to be away so long, I began to wonder if she'd ever reappear. Or if the whole thing – her talking to me and trying on necklaces – had been an illusion. Perhaps I was sick again and having some kind of hallucination.

But then – there she was – strolling back, taking her time.

When she was beside me, she sighed and said, 'Lovely garden, Logan. So interesting when a garden is allowed to go its own way. So much to find.'

My heart missed a beat with shock at the

way she spoke my language – so easily, so beautifully, *so intelligently.*

For that reason alone, I decided, I couldn't be delirious. Nothing could feel this good in a sick hallucination.

I glanced back at the house, afraid we were being watched. But it was still early on a Saturday. No one was up. No one looking out. All the curtains were still closed.

We walked together – she on four paws – gravitating towards the vegetable garden.

'You come here a lot, don't you?' she said when we reached the bench where last night's rug, torch and MP3 were still lying, each a little damp with overnight dew. 'You come here to talk to yourself. When there isn't anyone else who'll listen to your troubles. I've heard you.'

I giggled. 'I don't do it *aloud*, do I?'

'Perhaps not,' she said mysteriously. 'Though that doesn't mean I haven't heard.'

We sat close together on the bench and I started to ask the question I needed to ask…only it just wouldn't come out properly.

'Where did you…how can you…who are… I mean…'

'You sound like your father,' she said softly.

'All those unfinished sentences.'

Now she pointed it out, I knew I did — but how did she? She'd only met him for a few minutes last night. Still, it led us right on to the subject of Dad's inability to communicate with us — or anyone — and the way he shut himself away, composing weird, silence-filled music that almost no one wanted to listen to.

And this led to other things that troubled me in our family: Verity always getting what she wanted just through being pretty and adorable. Mum always worn out because in her words, '*I have to do just about everything in our household, including bring home most of the bacon.*'

In all my life, I realised, I'd never found anyone as easy to talk to as Tiff. I was so comfortable with her, I even let things out I hardly liked to admit to myself: how I never shone at anything, how I was just plain *nothing* at *everything*. How I longed to be really good at something, just one thing, like acting — acting most of all — but when I stood on the stage, or even stood up in class to recite a poem, my throat seemed to close and I couldn't breathe.

I told her about the friend stuff, about Cammy and Clarky now being stuck together with glue.

About how it was at school – always looking over your shoulder to see who was with you or against you.

At this, she expressed interest in coming to see for herself.

'They won't allow you in my school,' I assured her. 'Not ever. Not a pet.'

'Oh, we'll find a way,' said Tiff. 'You'll see.'

We'd been talking for such a while, it was no longer early. The autumn sun was already warm and the dew almost dry on the grass. And, of course, by now, everyone in the household *was* awake.

And next thing, Dad was out in the garden, calling my name.

My first thought was to answer. My second, remembering I was now impossible, was to hide, as in *Make Them Worry, Make Them Think I'd Run Away*.

Tiff was against it. 'They might come looking for you here. You don't want them finding out this is your secret place. Come, we'll go together and face the music.'

It seemed so right to take advice from Tiff so I bundled her up in my arms and we went to meet Dad.

He was pacing the lawn as he called for me, while

standing at the kitchen door was Bonyfingers, frowning and rattling her necklaces. Beside her was George, his face white and streaked with tears.

As we approached, George ran over and tried to stroke Tiff. 'It's no good. They won't let us keep you, Tiff Tunakins.'

'I'm sorry,' said Dad. 'We must take her to the Animal Rescue Home in Burton.'

'No!' I gasped, holding Tiff tighter.

'Her owner is probably mad with worry,' Dad said. 'If we don't try to reunite them it would be like…'

Bonyfingers said it for him. 'Stealing.'

I spluttered, 'But she hasn't got another owner. Look, where's her collar? She's a free cat who's come to *me*. You don't understand. She's different. She's mine. She's *meant* to be mine.'

'Sorry,' said Dad. He was being unusually stern. 'Your mother promised Mrs Everett there'd be no animals. We can't go back on that. So we're going to the Home right now before you get…'

Again Bonyfingers spoke for him, '*Too attached.*'

I scowled my most impossible scowl and snarled, 'Well, she's not going. Are you, Tiff?'

I looked straight into her eyes and she did her double blink, as if to say *put me down and I'll run.*

But Bonyfingers must have been anticipating this, expecting her to try to get away.

As I let her out of my arms and she touched the ground, Bonyfingers was on top of her – hurling herself in a most desperate way.

Now *she* held Tiff in her arms – tight – and was striding round the house towards Dad's car.

I ran after her to try to wrench Tiff back but Dad caught up with me, took my arm and bundled me into the back seat of the car.

'Now,' he said, 'are you going to behave and hold her yourself quietly or…' He paused, meeting my eyes dead on. 'Or do you want Mrs Everett to come with us?'

Well, ask a silly question. I didn't want Bonyfingers, the cat-hater, anywhere near me. I didn't want her touching my cat.

Scowling, I let her give me Tiff, and sat there clutching and stroking her as Dad drove us to Burton.

Several times she looked up and winked at me, both yellow eyes at once. When Dad pulled up in the Rescue Home car park, she put her paws on the edge of the window and examined her prison.

And then – she did the last thing I was expecting.

In front of my father she spoke out in her thrilling

film-star way, 'Don't worry about me. I'll be all right. I'm always all right. You'll see.'

Dad fixed us in the rear-view mirror.

'Was that...did she...that almost sounded as if...'

I grabbed my chance. 'She *did* speak, Dad. She said, "*Don't lock me up in this prison, PLEASE.*"'

He smiled and turned round to look at us. 'You're quite a kid, Logie. You really are. You just made that up, didn't you? Come on. Let's do this thing before you...uh...convince me...'

Inside the Home, at reception, we were asked lots of questions. Between them, Dad and the receptionist filled in some forms and Dad signed them.

They were all very kind in there, of course, being animal-lovers. More animal-lovers than people-lovers, I should think. But they could see my distress and tried to comfort me with words I knew weren't true in Tiff's case...things like *it'll be best for the cat, it's for her sake, we're taking her in*.

And so, I stood by helplessly as Tiff was locked up in a cage on the cat wing in Burton's Rescue Home.

While Dad paced a short distance away, giving me space to say goodbye, I stroked her nose through the bars.

'Why didn't you scratch and bite Bonyfingers

when she had you, jump out of her arms and run for it?' I said.

'I don't scratch and bite,' she answered. 'I'm not that kind of a cat.'

Then, after a bit more stroking she said softly, 'Don't worry, this is not goodbye. You think I'm your cat and I am your cat. I'll be back with you before long.'

I told her I'd come and visit her if I could.

'Good,' she said, 'then bring tuna cakes cooked with a little potato, and don't forget parsley. The food in here is bound to be terrible. Oh, and leave me your telephone number. In case I get a chance to call you.'

I ran to the reception desk to beg paper and pen, scribbled down my mobile number and pushed it through the bars of the cage.

Tiff hid it under her water dish. 'I'll memorise it later and then eat the paper,' she said – making me giggle, even in those circumstances! 'Now, go on, be off with you, I need a nap and besides, your father is getting agitated.'

Back in the car, before he turned on the ignition, Dad fixed me with his eyes. 'And what was she saying there at the end, before you…uh…ran back to reception?'

I tried him with the truth. 'She said, "give me your number so I can call you if I get the chance."'

That made him do something I'd never heard him do. He gave a big, fat, wonderful laugh.

# Chapter 11

# BONYFINGERS LIES AND I SET OUT TO PROVE IT

Big fat wonderful laugh or not, when we got home, Dad put his DO NOT DISTURB sign up on his study door and withdrew.

Bonyfingers tried to behave as if nothing had happened.

She tried to be nice to me.

The nicer she was, the ruder I was back, never answering her questions, turning my back on her, sighing and snarling horrid things about her under my breath so she had to purse her lips closed to stop herself snapping. (Another fat red tick for No 8 on The List.)

That night I dreamed Tiff escaped from the Burton Home and got run over and I was out on my bike and found her by the side of the road.

I woke up crying because she was so real in the dream and though she was dead she wasn't dead. With her pink insides showing – all very clean and neat, I must say – she'd lifted her head and said, 'Don't worry. You think I'm your cat because I am your cat, and dead doesn't mean I'm not alive.'

All Sunday I stayed in my room, watching my mobile, now on 24/7 in case Tiff called as she'd said she might. And not doing my weekend homework so I could put a fat red tick against No 13 on The Impossible List.

I didn't even touch my theatre. Just lay on my unmade bed, staring at The List on the wall and wondering how I was going to get through the days. Without Mum. Without Verity. Without Cammy unsticking herself from Clarky. And now without the one thing that could have made up for no Mum and no Verity, and no best friend: Tiff.

Tiff, who could talk my language. Tiff, who promised mystery and excitement and attention, which I so longed for. Tiff, who already understood me better than anyone on earth, even though she'd just walked into my life.

By the end of Sunday, after all that lying around – and no call from Tiff – I decided it was time to tick No 9 on The List, as in: *Don't come home straight after school at least three times a week.*

Not coming home, on the school bus, straight after school – unless there had been prior agreement with Mum (and now, I supposed, Mrs Everett or Dad) – was absolutely the most forbidden thing to do in our family. Even for Paul and Verity.

Great, I thought. All the more reason to do it – the very next day, Monday. Extra great because I had somewhere worthwhile to go: the Barton Animal Rescue Home! *To see Tiff!*

The decision got me up off my bed and downstairs to organise *'tuna cakes cooked with potato and parsley'* as per Tiff's request and to borrow some money from Paul for *'the Book Sale at school'* – really for the bus fare to and from Burton.

To be further impossible, I set about making the tuna cakes right there in the kitchen while Bonyfingers was preparing our supper. Deliberately getting in her way.

I made as much mess as I could and even removed one of the pans she was cooking something in, to make way for my pot of potatoes on the cooker.

Everything she said, I ignored, humming quietly to myself, as if there were no one else in the kitchen but me. When she spoke more loudly, I only hummed more loudly.

Eventually, though, when Tiff's cakes were done (without parsley, as there wasn't any I could find) and our supper was on the table and Paul and George came in, I stopped humming and Bonyfingers took her chance and said, 'Are you going to share those fish cakes with us, or eat them yourself?'

Stupidly, stupidly, I couldn't resist saying – or rather snarling – '*They-fr-Tiff.*' And then adding, because I realised my mistake, '*Case-she-cmes-back.*'

But it was too late to cover up. Paul and Bonyfingers looked at me as if they thought I was up to something. And with a sinking heart, I realised I'd probably blown it, given it away that I *was somehow expecting to see Tiff.*

And Bonyfingers must have guessed the rest – guessed I was planning to visit Tiff – because the next day when school ended, there she was at the school gates. Watching out with her glittering hawk eyes.

She didn't even wait for me to get *through* the gates before she pounced and hustled me to her rusty car.

George was already sitting in it, collected from his school because he was too young to catch the bus home by himself.

He caught my eye, as if he knew what was going on, then turned and stared sadly out the window.

66

As Bonyfingers started the car and we rattled too fast down the rutted road, nearly killing two strutting crows, she said without looking at me, 'I'll be fetching you every day from now on, Logan. I might as well come straight on from collecting George. It's not far. It's no trouble.'

I said nothing and when we got home I took Tiff's tuna cakes wrapped in foil from my lunchbox and threw them in the kitchen bin. Though I didn't give Paul back the '*book sale*' money he'd lent me.

On Tuesday and Wednesday I let Bonyfingers collect me, not saying a word, not even to George who was sitting beside me staring out of the window, wrapped in his own silence.

On Thursday I told my teacher I had to leave school fifteen minutes early (using Mum being away and me having to walk round to George's school to fetch him as an excuse).

I was out of the school gates well before Bonyfingers *should* have been there – and hurrying down the road to the next bus stop (where I knew I could get a bus to Letford, which wasn't that far from Burton).

Only suddenly, from out of nowhere, there she was – screeching up in her rusty car, coming to a stop right beside me.

67

I started to run but she jumped out of the car and came after me. She caught up only because I stumbled over a clump of something or other.

'So where do you think you are going, young lady?' she panted, as she gripped my arm like a vice and marched me back to the car.

When I didn't answer she continued, 'I can guess, Logan. Burton and the Animal Rescue Home.'

Then she changed her tack completely. 'You know, you're upsetting little George with your behaviour. Me too, of course, but that doesn't matter as much as it matters that you're distressing George. Why are you doing this, Logan? Your mother would be most disappointed to hear of it. So, why?'

I could see George's anxious face inside the car, pressed against the window, trying to hear what was going on.

I decided to say something intelligible, just this once, a last-ditch attempt to make her get it.

'I miss Tiff,' I said, looking her straight in the eye. 'I want her back. You don't understand, she's not someone else's cat. She came to our house, *for me.*'

Bonyfingers sighed and shook her head. 'No, Logan. She is not yours and you know that very well. You found her in the garden. She cannot be yours.'

She opened the car door and waited for me to get in.

I considered running for it again, but George's face stopped me.

I got in and we drove home in silence.

And then, the next day, just before supper, she did what she should not have done, what no grown-up should ever do to a child. She told me A WHOPPER – A Great Big Cruel Lie That Pushed Me Over The Edge.

'The Rescue Home telephoned,' she said, 'while you were at school. Tiff's owner has claimed her.'

I felt sure it was a lie the minute she said it. I felt sure because I knew Tiff didn't have an owner *to* claim her. Tiff had made it clear enough. She was her own owner. She gave herself to whoever she chose.

And because of the cruel whopper – which I was sure was a lie but which also brought a tingle of fear that it wasn't and that Tiff *had* been claimed by someone – I made new resolutions:

1) I would go to the Rescue Home and PROVE IT ONE WAY OR ANOTHER.
2) It would no longer be a case of grunting and sneering and not answering when I was spoken to. Now it would be a case of NOT SAYING

69

ANYTHING AT ALL. EVER. I would become Completely Silent. That would teach her. Teach them all.

Only it isn't easy to be silent of your own free will. The natural thing when someone speaks to you is to look at their mouths and engage. Once you've done that, you answer automatically. You just do.

So I stopped looking at mouths. I disengaged. No words reached me because I wasn't available to receive them. They floated around, nothing to do with me, not my affair. It was as if I'd climbed into a space capsule.

From the capsule – for the rest of Friday – I saw my silence driving Bonyfingers mad and rejoiced. She had this coming to her – and the rest.

Saturday morning I was up early before anyone else had stirred. I didn't leave a note on purpose. *Worry about me. Worry*, I thought. *Think I've run away.*

I turned off my phone so they couldn't get hold of me and set off for the bus stop, for Burton and the Rescue Home.

Of course, I was not allowed to go into town by myself. Another House Rule of the Sacred Variety. Good, I thought. When I get home I'll be able to tick No 2 on The List, *Do the opposite of what you're told*, and No 3, *Do dangerous things that make them sick with worry.*

The bus was filled with people going to the Burton Saturday market. I had to stand all the way. One woman started making me her business. 'Are you all right, love?' she said. 'On your own, love? Where you going on your own, love?'

She meant well, of course. She told me her name was Marge Griffin. Her cat had died of old age and she couldn't live without one so she was going to get a replacement from the Rescue Home.

*She's not getting Tiff, that is for sure*, I kept thinking, *so I'd better not let her out of my sight.*

I decided it was OK to come out of my silent capsule when I wasn't with the family – and told her I was going to the Home too.

She didn't ask why and we walked together from the bus stop – me saying nothing – she not noticing because she was talking non-stop about first her husband dying and then her cat and everything coming in threes and who would be next.

At the Home the doors were just opening. We were the first people there. What I hadn't thought of was how I was going to get past reception. You can't just go wandering in to the animal cages at a Rescue Home. You have to declare yourself and your intentions at the desk.

Luckily, there was only one man behind the desk

71

this early and he hadn't been there when Dad and I had brought Tiff in.

Thanking the stars for Marge Griffin, I hung around beside her, doing my best to look as if we belonged together.

When she'd got permission to go through to the cat wing, I went along too, staying as close to her as I dared.

And there, exactly where I'd last seen her, as big and black as ever, not claimed by any other owner, was Tiff – living proof Bonyfingers *had lied*.

Her nose was jutting through two bars and her eyes were closed.

'*Tiff. Tiff*,' I whispered as I walked up.

Her yellow eyes sprang open. Then, startled only for a moment, she stretched and said softly, 'Logie! What a lovely surprise! Did you bring the fish cakes?'

Her thrilling voice that I hadn't imagined!

'No, no fish cakes,' I whispered back excitedly. 'Bonyfingers told me you'd been claimed by your owner. I've come to take you home and prove she's a big cruel liar.'

'About time,' said Tiff. 'There's been no chance of escape. And two families have attempted to adopt me. I had to behave very badly to put them off. Hissing and spitting. So against my nature. So undignified.'

Marge Griffin came bustling up. 'My, now here's a handsome creature. And you can see at once, a most intelligent pussy. Aren't you, you beauty.'

'She's my cat,' I gabbled. 'The one I've come to claim. You can't have her.'

At this, Marge suddenly focused – as if only now realising I'd come in with her and becoming suspicious. 'Does your mother know you're here?' she asked, frowning.

'No, she's in Australia.'

'Your father?'

'No, he's in his study and can't be disturbed. But she is my cat, I promise, Mrs Griffin.'

Marge scratched at her hair.

'Well, I doubt they'll let someone your age sign out a cat,' she said. 'So if I was you I'd get your father out of his study and down here to claim the cat for you. That is my advice, love.'

I nodded and waited for her to go on her way, peering into each cage looking for an ideal cat replacement.

To Tiff I said, 'So how will I get you out?'

'I'm already thinking about that,' said Tiff. 'It will have to involve her. That Mrs Griffin. She's a good sort, one can tell. She'll help. So here's the plan.'

## Chapter 12

# TIFF GOES FREE AND I GET CAUGHT RED-HANDED

Even though my throat closes and I can't breathe when I'm on stage in front of an audience – off stage, I'd say I'm a natural actress. And as per Tiff's plan I went up to Marge, sobbing convincingly, 'I've called my father, Mrs Griffin, and he's working and won't come down here and claim my cat. So will you help me spend a little time with her? I mean, I've come all this way. Can you ask if we can take her into the visitors' room? I miss her so much. Please.'

She was a kind, cat-loving woman, Marge Griffin, or she wouldn't have been in that Home in the first place. So this part of the plan worked easily enough.

She regarded me for a moment, pushed my hair back gently and said, 'Well, I can't see it'll do any harm. So all right, love, but only if you'll stop your weeping. Can't bear to see a young thing like you cry.'

I brightened and she found me a tissue in her bag and bustled off to find a warden. I crossed my fingers that whoever she came back with wouldn't recognise me from when Dad and I brought Tiff in.

And, after what seemed like an eternity of worrying, Marge returned with a woman warden who hadn't been on duty that time and didn't know me from Adam, or I suppose I should say Eve.

So far so good.

She unlocked Tiff's cage and carried her into the visitors' room. There she handed her to Marge and Marge gave her to me.

I sat down and Tiff made herself at home in my arms, purring as usual like a motorbike.

'My,' said the warden. 'She likes you. She's been quite spiteful to other children who've tried to hold her. Strange how they take to some and not to others.'

'Oh yes,' said Marge, 'animals know where they belong all right.'

The warden smiled, jangled the keys at her belt and turned to straighten notices on the bulletin board.

I stroked Tiff and muttered sweet nothings for a bit.

Then I got up with her in my arms and said to the warden, 'I need to go to the toilet. It's urgent.'

Surprised, the warden said, 'Well, you can't take the cat with you, dear. Give her to your grandmother.'

Marge blushed and I realised this was the deception she'd used in order to get a warden to show us Tiff. She'd said she was my grandmother!

She shuffled towards me, nervously – not liking the idea of deceiving a good Rescue warden, I could see – and said, 'I'll hold her, love, while you go.'

The warden took the keys from her belt and slid one into the lock in the door.

I was aware I had to time the next bit perfectly.

As the warden pulled the latch, I moved, very slightly, as if to give Tiff to Marge – yet without loosening my hold.

Then, as soon as the door started to open, I quickly bent down and let her out of my arms.

In a flash, she was away through the gap, streaking down the short corridor into and then across the reception area – which was now filling up with claimers and savers and animals to be saved.

To the cries of the warden and Marge, I tore after her, dodging everyone as best I could and finally throwing my weight against the glass entrance doors to open them.

Tiff, who was already there waiting for me to do this as agreed, shot through the doors and was gone.

I followed and immediately tripped.

Tiff was free, all right, but I was lying on the concrete step outside the Home, my shoulder throbbing.

The warden and the receptionist were soon bending over me, trying to help me up – Marge, panting and clutching her heart, behind them.

They wanted to take me inside and check I was all right. But I could see the warden was not pleased and, quite rightly, most suspicious of the whole incident.

I was not a fast runner but was going to have to be now.

I gave Marge a look that I hoped said both 'thank you' and 'sorry', and ran.

Tiff and I had agreed she would turn right out of the entrance and I would turn left. Then we'd both lie low for an hour before meeting at the statue in the market square. Then we'd go home together on the bus and gather everyone in the kitchen – and present the evidence that Mrs Everett was a cruel *liar*. I just couldn't wait to see her face.

But in my panic, I forgot that's what we'd agreed and just ran – any which way, I didn't know – making for Burton's narrowest streets and back alleys, running till my lungs were bursting and a stitch ached in my side.

Then I sat down in the doorway of a pub that was

boarded up – in a cobbled road that was more of a path than anything and quite deserted – got my breath back and turned on my mobile to find out the time.

There was another half-hour to go before I should be in the square. There were also two messages from Paul asking where I was and telling me to call him urgently. Good. Good, good, I thought, turning the phone off.

I spent the next twenty minutes studying the graffiti on the boarded-up pub. (It was on my Impossible List to do some where it would most offend.)

Then I made my way to the square and the statue – easily enough, since anyone I asked could direct me.

Tiff wasn't there.

Three hours I waited and she didn't arrive.

I sat, imagining she'd been recaptured by the Rescue Home or run over as in my dream.

And then, suddenly, it was me who was being caught...by surprise, and in the grip of a stern-faced policewoman.

# Chapter 13
## MEETING TROUBLE WITH SILENCE

With one hand round my arm, and fingering her radio with the other, she said, 'Hello, dear. Here for the market, are you?'

I nodded.

'Alone?'

I nodded.

'What's your name?'

I said nothing – pulling down my silent capsule – and gazing off into the distance.

She continued. 'A girl about your age and description is missing from home. Her family is worried.' She consulted her notepad. 'Logan Dempster?'

I said nothing. Looking over her shoulder, I scanned the square for Tiff.

The policewoman waited patiently. Then, after

examining my face for a while, 'You are required to tell me your name.'

She talked into her crackly radio and then repeated herself. 'Your name? You are required to tell me.'

And that was the moment I made up my mind to really run away. Not just make them worry, to make them think I had. And it didn't matter where to, either. London, Scotland, South America for all I cared.

I don't think she was expecting me to break for it – and by now she'd loosened her grip on my arm.

I was easily away from her and haring across the square, ducking and diving between the market stalls, making back to the narrow alleys.

But policewomen are fit. They probably spend all their free time in gyms. She caught up with me before I was even out of the square.

Her grip was tighter this time. She marched me back to her car – all the stall holders and the shoppers falling silent as we went.

In the car, she locked the doors – remotely. There was more crackly radio talk. I heard her 'roger and over' that she probably had Logan Dempster.

We set off over the bumpy cobbles.

And there, through the window of that police car I saw Tiff, sauntering past some shops – as if she had all day – towards the pedestrian crossing that led into the square.

I shouted, 'Stop. There she is!'

The policewoman did stop, ramming on the brake.

'Who, who is there? Where?' she said, straining to look around.

'There, crossing the road,' I yelled. 'My cat! My cat! Let me out. I've got to get to her.'

I rattled the door and beat my fists on the window glass.

'Calm down, dear. I can't see any cat. Where is the cat?'

I started to cry because (1) try as I might, I was not a natural criminal and (2) because she was right: Tiff had vanished again.

'I must get you home,' the policewoman said, putting her hand up to stroke my hair but thinking better of it. 'Now, come on. You are Logan Dempster, aren't you? You fit her description exactly.'

I nodded. She sighed, let off the brake and set off for our house – talking into her radio – knowing the way without asking me.

As we pulled into the drive, Dad came out to meet us.

I caught a glimpse of Bonyfingers hovering just outside the open front door. She looked distraught and

I was glad. *Good,* I thought. *Not as distraught as you should be, Liar.*

Dad told me to wait while he talked with the policewoman.

I stood nearby kicking gravel and trying to listen but they spoke too quietly for me to hear anything.

Then he thanked her for bringing me home safely and ushered me upstairs.

We sat on my bed in the middle of the tip that my room now was. I played with my phone, as Dad went on and on in his half-finished way: *It was irresponsible to do what I'd done. And the fright I'd given them. Poor Mrs Everett.* (What? She was the cause of it.) *And wasting police time. Did I know it was an offence? And anyway, what did I think I was doing and why?*

I sat through it all, half in and half out of my silent capsule. His words interested me – coming from him who, protected by Mum, had never had to tell off one of his children before. But they didn't make me want to defend myself. I kept silent, not looking at him, fiddling with my phone – vaguely hoping Tiff might call.

Dad got up and paced the room, stopping in front of my theatre, drawing a curtain to and fro in an absent-minded way.

Then he looked up at me and said, 'The police officer said you mentioned a cat. Your cat. You went to visit it – her – didn't you, at the Rescue Home? You must tell me, Logan.'

I nodded my head slowly and, at the mention of Tiff, burst into tears again.

He wanted to take me in his arms and comfort me, I could tell. He didn't because he didn't know how. Instead he patted my back and offered to send Paul up.

At the door he cleared his throat. 'Logie, I know you're upset about...uh...everything. Not being allowed to keep that cat...your mother being away. But it doesn't change anything. You broke the rules...going into town like that. I believe your mother...well, she's not here...so I'm going to have to...'

He was going to say, 'ground you,' I was sure, but he couldn't finish the sentence. Pity, because if he had grounded me, I could have gone out anyway, and then ticked No 5 on The List.

He melted away and after a bit Paul came knocking.

He hadn't come to comfort me though. He was furious: *I'd put them through so much – what was I thinking, going off like that without telling anyone?*

I kept my silent capsule slammed tight, thinking: *Go away, Paul, I cannot hear you.*

Soon after he did go, Bonyfingers came knocking.

Dad must have told her I'd been to Burton to see Tiff because, if you ask me, she was dripping with guilt. As if she knew I'd only done it to check whether Tiff had been claimed as she'd alleged. As if she knew it was all her fault.

She didn't tut at the mess in my room, though I could see she was shocked. *Good.*

She asked if I'd like a cup of tea. Then she admired my necklaces – the ones Tiff had been trying on – still spread out on the dressing table. This so got on my nerves I nearly screamed.

But I didn't. I stayed in my capsule and let her suffer through my silence.

Next she oohed and aahed over my model theatre. 'Do you like the theatre?' she asked. (*Well, what do you think, you lying old hag, that's why I'm making a model one,* I replied in my head.) She suggested we might go and see a play together at the Burton Playhouse.

I considered miming vomiting.

I so hated her in my room.

I did not look at her once. Waiting for her to say something *to the point* and *admit* she'd lied.

86

To APOLOGISE for it.

She did nothing of the sort. Only frittered on about nothing, trying to make friends!

When at last she left, I sat in a huddle on my bed, hugging my secret weapon to myself: I had proof she was a Cruel Liar and I'd use that weapon when the moment was right.

And then I sat up straight in sudden shock as, like an icy wind, the truth of the situation blew through me: I *didn't* have proof. There was no Tiff to present in the kitchen as evidence Bonyfingers was a big fat liar. No Tiff with me and no Tiff in the Animal Rescue Home! She might as well have been 'claimed by her owner' for all I could prove.

I was back where I'd started. No Mum, no Verity, no Cammy, no Tiff, no proof of Bonyfingers' cruel lying, no anything.

I still had Being Impossible though. And the Weapon of Silence. And for the next six days I stayed inside my capsule, driving them all mad.

Finally, the next Saturday morning, Paul came to see me – Dad sent him, I'm sure.

I was painting some scenery for the theatre – actually a doll's house table and two chairs.

'Logie Bogie,' he cajoled, crouching down and examining the theatre as if he were really interested.

'This thing is brilliant. You're such a little craftsperson.'

He turned my face to him and I could smell the chewing gum on his breath, 'You've got to come out of this silent thing,' he said. 'Dad thinks it's because of that cat. Because it had to go to the Rescue Home. But that's ridiculous, Logie. It was only a stray. You only had it for what…one night? It's not like it was yours or ours for years or anything. I mean how could you be so upset about losing a cat you'd only…well…borrowed…for a few hours? And another thing. It's not Bonyfingers' fault she's here. Mum employed her and it's not Mum's fault either. She had to go to Grandad. He's old and frail and now with his hip, he needs her. You can't mind about it. As for Vee, it is selfish of her to go to Farah's, and I'm going to call her and tell her she has to come back.'

Some of what he said was true, of course, but I didn't acknowledge it. Just stared, as if I hadn't heard a word.

He had one more go. 'If you don't start talking soon, Logie, we…we all think you should see a doctor.'

I picked up one of the doll's house chairs and started painting its legs.

'Tell you what,' he said. 'Tomorrow's Sunday.

I'll ring Vee and make sure she comes home for lunch. She'll sort you out. Bring you out of this.' And he left.

I picked up my phone, willing Tiff to ring. *Ring, Tiff, ring. If you memorised my phone number, as you said you would, you should still remember it. Ring and tell me where you are.*

*At least let me know you're safe.*

The phone gave me the same silent treatment I was giving my family.

I lay on my bed in the silence and imagined the play I might put on in my theatre when it was finished. A play about a house with no proper foundations. A house slowly sinking into the marshy earth below and taking the people who lived there with it. By the end of the play the house would be practically sunk – its occupants living *on the roof*. Refusing to admit they're going down with the house. Cheerful, as they camp amongst the bits of furniture they'd managed to haul up there. Cooking on a primus stove and sleeping in one bed under the stars whatever the weather. Carrying on as if nothing unusual were happening.

I smiled – for the first time, probably, since Mum had left – wondering how it would end. This play – about my family.

Maybe a huge black cat who could talk so you understood her would come in and lead them to safer ground. But only after she made them admit they were sinking.

# Chapter 14
## MY MOBILE RINGS BUT IS IT TIFF?

I stayed up late writing some dialogue for the play.

So far I had three characters: Mr Dumpster, Mrs Dumpster and their completely ugly fat daughter, Verisimilitude Dumpster, who thinks she's beautiful! (I'd looked Verity up in the dictionary and found verisimilitude just above it. It means 'seeming like the truth'. Perfect for my purposes.)

I had Mr Dumpster being a car salesman, Mrs Dumpster a window-dresser and Verisimilitude so fat she couldn't walk or go to school so she sat all day stuffing her face, weighing the house down further into the mud. (Good, the real Verity eats nothing.)

In the dialogue I had them talking about a new car Mr Dumpster can't sell (he is a bad salesman but according to him it is the fault of the merchandise).

And about a new range of expensive models' clothes Mrs Dumpster is putting in a window which she thinks will look perfect on Verisimilitude. And all the time they talk, the house is crumbling and sinking into the mire.

It made me laugh. Yes, my own made-up dialogue cheered me right up. Revenge can do that.

I was so cheered, my thoughts turned to Gerald. *The boy genius electronics wizard.* How soon, I wondered, would I have the courage to ask if he'd get the lights working in my theatre and – maybe, why not – the front-of-stage curtains opening and closing at the press of a button?

It needed to be soon. It had to be soon. Or I'd sink into the mud of my own lonely misery.

It was well after one in the morning when I eventually fell asleep and the next thing I knew was George jumping on my bed in great excitement. 'Come on, wake up! I'll tell you what's happening.'

I sat up and George – bouncing throughout – brought me the news.

'Vee is coming for lunch. Today. This today. And she's going to make you talk again. And I'm very pleased because I hate you not talking. And you know what else?'

He jumped off the bed, landing in a heap on

the floor, hurting himself, then hopping on the leg that wasn't hurt.

'Bonyfingers is taking Mimi downstairs to clean her cage,' he gabbled away, ninety kilometres an hour. 'Paul says about time too as the house is beginning to smell. I asked her if I can help. First she looked cross. Then she said all right why not because I'd asked so nicely. And I *had* asked nicely because I really want to get to know that bird. It is a parrot and parrots are interesting.'

He continued hopping, full of excitement. And I was filled with such love for him that it hurt. If anyone could make me climb out of my silent capsule it was him – not Verity.

I crooked my finger to call him closer and hugged him hard. It was uncomfortable, as if the walls of my capsule were banging against his ears.

He struggled out of the hug – anxious to get on with the cage cleaning and getting to know Mimi.

He wanted me to help too, he said. He thought it would be better if I did. So would I *please* get up and come down?

For George – beloved George – I broke silence.

'Yes,' I said. 'I will. For you. Because I love you.'

He left at a run, shouting as he hurtled down the stairs, 'She spoke to me. Logie spoke to me!'

And now, for George, I jumped out of bed.

I'd finished pulling on one leg of an old pair of jeans when my phone rang.

I felt sure it was Tiff. The ring rang differently. It hummed the air like an electric current.

I hopped, one leg in and one out of the jeans, over to my phone. I didn't check the number of who was calling. It wasn't going to be a number already in my phone.

Hairs prickled on the back of my neck. I fumbled – nearly dropping the phone – clicked answer and said, 'TIFF?'

I heard something. Surely, her deep thrilling voice, starting to speak to me. Then a fluffing. A human voice in the background and the phone went down.

I found the number in received calls and dialled it. It rang for a bit then a man's voice answered, 'Dryboard Hardware. Can I help you?'

What could I say? *Excuse me, did a cat just try to use your phone? Because if so, she was calling me.*

I clicked off, deciding I was being ridiculous. Tiff was never going to phone, even if she had memorised my number. How could she? From where? On whose telephone?

I threw my mobile onto the bed and went downstairs to help George.

## Chapter 15

# MIMI GOES FOR GEORGE AND TIFF FLIES IN

Bonyfingers had put Mimi in the garden shed for the cage-cleaning operation.

The empty cage was in the middle of the lawn. George was hosing it out wearing oversized rubber gloves.

Whooping with delight, he was flapping his extended fingers, flushing Mimi's old dry droppings into the grass where they lay like hundreds of small white stars in a green slushy sky.

Some of them were so firmly stuck to the bottom of the cage they wouldn't budge and were going to have to be scrubbed away.

Bonyfingers brought a bucket of hot soapy water. She tried to hand me a wire-wool brush and a pair of gloves – her bracelets clacking like a pack of geese.

'This can be your little job, Logan,' she said. 'It will do you good to do something physical.'

Her thinking she knew what would do me good made my blood boil.

I was so boiling I couldn't help myself – even if I didn't have the proof.

Lifting its invisible lid, I stepped out of my silent capsule, and yelled, '*Liar!*'

George spun round with the shock of it and sprayed me with the hose.

Bonyfingers' eyes bulged so hard I thought they were going to pop out of her head.

I waited for her to say something like: *What do you mean, 'liar'? How dare you speak to me like that!*

She didn't. She just stared at me with a sad, haunted expression that told me she knew exactly what I was talking about.

Then she shivered, as if with disbelief at the situation she found herself in, rattled her necklaces and again offered me the brush and gloves, saying, 'Come along, Logan. Let it go. Let it be. The cat thing. It's over and done with. Give Mimi's cage a scrubbing while I pop down to the store. We need a few things for lunch. It will be nice to see your sister, won't it? And your father intends to join us too. That'll be something in itself.

Pity the oven's so grungy. The fumes will flavour the roast.'

She dropped the brush into the soapy water, draped the gloves on the side of the bucket and jangled her way back to the house.

George ran after her.

'Mrs Everett,' he asked in his irresistible way. 'Can I go in the shed and see Mimi. I'd love to see her out of her cage and flying around. I never saw a parrot flying in real life before.'

Bonyfingers stiffened. She was quite firm. 'No, George. You most certainly cannot go into the shed. Mimi isn't used to company except mine. If you want to watch her, watch through the shed window.'

George nodded, disappointed but not arguing.

We waited for Bonyfingers to disappear inside.

'I bet she'd like some company though,' said George quietly. 'That parrot's probably got to be the way she is from not having more people around.'

He looked longingly at the shed, then shrugged and said, 'So are you going to scrub the cage or shall I?'

'I'll do it,' I replied. (I'd broken my silence now and was glad to get back to talking, relieved that I still knew how.) 'You go and watch

Mimi through the window.'

'OK,' said George. 'And please don't be silent any more, Logie. It's so scary.'

I tousled his hair and got down in the grass to work on the stuck droppings on the cage floor.

And it *was* good to be doing something physical – Bonyfingers was right there. I gave myself up to the foaming work while George peered in the grimy shed window. I could hear him tapping on the glass and calling Mimi's name.

I was not watching when he went in. (Though – thinking back – I probably did hear him turn the key in the shed door lock.)

Later he told me why he'd gone in: Mimi was coming up to the window, perching on a clay pot and cocking her head to one side. She was being friendly, he said. For once he'd just had to do what he'd been told not to. He just *had* to.

And now I certainly heard him yelling his head off – and Mimi squawking as if a hawk were eating her chicks.

I dropped the scrubbing brush and hared over.

Luckily, George hadn't closed the door properly behind him.

I pulled it open quickly enough and saw Mimi going for him.

'Get out!' I screamed, holding the door open for him.

He backed out and started to run.

But I wasn't quick enough and didn't slam the door in time.

Mimi was through it and after George.

I yelled at him to make for the house but Mimi was already diving for him and he was so terrified he was running – not towards safety, but in panicky circles on the lawn, trying to beat her off with his arms.

The noise the three of us were making was so loud you'd think it would have brought Dad and Paul running. Yet no one came.

I spotted a rake by the side of the house, dashed for it, and swung it round in the air, trying to beat Mimi away with the handle.

She easily swooped out of reach of every swipe and continued diving at George.

And then he tripped over his own feet and fell.

I yelled, 'Crawl, George, crawl to the kitchen.'

He got onto his knees and elbows and began to inch across the grass.

All the time Mimi kept on circling and diving.

The rake and I were useless to stop her.

I remembered the hose. It could be George's last

chance. I ran to the tap to turn it on full force.

As I dashed, Mimi struck.

Her beak went right through George's shorts and the skin on his backside.

He spun round with the pain and fell back, now exposing his face.

I screamed at him to cover it – which he instinctively did with his hands anyway, as anyone would.

So Mimi went for his hands.

And all I could think was: *If I don't drown her with the hose, she'll get past his hands and peck his eyes out.* But though I'd turned on the tap, I still had to get to the nozzle, which was lying in the grass.

I ran for where I thought George had left it but, in my panic, couldn't find it and then saw what was coming: *a bundle of black fur – streaking across the garden.*

*Tiff.*

She took a flying leap. There was a momentary airborne ball of furious fur, feathers and squawking.

Then Tiff was walking away, and Mimi was lying in the grass near George – dead.

In my amazement, I did not notice I was spraying Verity with the hose…Verity, coming out of the kitchen door…arriving, of course, after she was needed, after there was any chance of having her loveliness smudged by the darker side of life.

'Hey! Get that off me!' she called, moving gracefully on her willow-wand legs, like an angel of mercy, towards the sobbing George.

# Chapter 16

## GEORGE GOES TO HOSPITAL AND MIMI'S MUMMIFIED

I don't remember exactly how or from where – maybe Verity went to get them – but it didn't take long before everyone was there. Paul down from his room, Dad out from his study. Bonyfingers back from shopping.

An ambulance arrived, the paramedics leaping out of it, running through the house to where George still lay on the grass, the Angel of Sudden Mercy soothing him.

Dead Mimi had been removed – taken away, no doubt, by Bonyfingers.

The paramedics examined George before putting him on a stretcher. 'The trauma is probably worse than his wounds, which are mostly skin deep,' I heard one of them tell Dad. 'But, as parrots can carry diseases that transmit to humans, he will need to have some tests.'

Dad, white as a sheet, followed them as they took the stretchered George to the ambulance and got into the back to go to the hospital with him.

Doors slammed, the siren wailed, and they were off down the drive.

Now Paul took charge.

He asked me for 'A full account of what happened.'

(First, I demanded a full account of why neither he nor Dad had heard our screams and come to help. Paul said he couldn't speak for Dad but he was upstairs listening to music with his earphones on.)

As soon as I'd explained everything as I knew it to him and Vee, he gave Verity the job of phoning Mum in Melbourne and telling her. 'Without giving her a heart attack,' he warned.

Then he made a cup of tea for Bonyfingers, who was on the sofa in the sitting room rocking herself and moaning, dead Mimi in her lap. He stood in front of her, offering the tea. She didn't take it, just rocked and moaned softly.

He came out and said he thought he'd better call our doctor and disappeared to do so.

In a way, I was the best off. I had Tiff back, purring like a motorbike in my lap.

We sat at the bottom of the stairs from where we (Tiff and I) could see Bonyfingers rocking in the sitting room and listen to Verity talking to Mum on the phone in the hall.

'Mum, something's happened,' she said calmly. 'George has gone to hospital. But he's all right. He will be fine.'

I could faintly hear Mum on the other end, screeching.

Verity explained more. 'Mrs Everett's parrot attacked him, so he's pecked and bleeding but the parrot didn't get his eyes, which it was trying to. Dad's gone with him to hospital and he'll be there for a bit because of the danger of parrot diseases but he is OK. Just sore and very shocked.'

'Tell her about Tiff,' I urged. 'Tell her it was Tiff who saved him.'

Vee ignored my request and instead, with a sob welling under her light voice, she said, 'Can you come home, Mum? Please?'

'Well?' I cried, when she put the phone down. 'Is she coming?'

'She'll be on the next plane she can. She has to sort out a few things for Grandad first.'

Vee sat beside me on the step and stroked Tiff.

'How did she come to be here?' she asked. 'Paul rang me and said you'd found a cat in the garden but that Dad had made you take it to the Rescue Home in Burton.'

'I freed her yesterday,' I said quietly. 'That's why I went to Burton.'

'Oh, yes!' she frowned at me. 'Paul told me about that too. He said you'd sneaked off alone without letting anyone know where you were – and that they'd had to tell the police. You shouldn't have done that, Logie. Why didn't you call me? I'd have gone with you.'

'Would you?' I said bitterly. 'Or would you have been too busy having a good time at Farah's?'

Tiff stopped purring and said clearly, 'Don't you two fight. I'm only sorry I didn't get to George sooner.'

'Did you hear that?' I asked Vee. 'She says we mustn't fight and she's sorry she didn't get here sooner.'

Verity's tears dried as mild irritation took over. 'Paul was right, Logie. You're going off your head. Cats purr and mew, they don't talk. You need Mum home to bring you to your senses. We all do.'

She got up. 'I want to go to the hospital. I'll call Fa and ask if her Mum can take me.'

The doorbell rang. It was Dr Shaw, our doctor and

a friend of Mum's — I'd known him all my life.

Paul came out of the kitchen and they shook hands.

Dr Shaw said how sorry he was about the 'incident' (which Paul had obviously explained on the phone) and offered me something for 'the shock'.

I said I didn't need anything because I had Tiff.

Paul indicated Bonyfingers rocking and moaning in the sitting room.

Dr Shaw nodded and suggested we kids go upstairs while he had a chat with her. Vee and Paul went. I didn't. I hung about on the staircase so I could listen in and watch.

I saw and heard Dr Shaw offering Mrs E something for *her* shock. She turned it down too.

He sat beside her on the sofa and told her gently that there were some serious issues at stake here. 'So the more you can tell me about what happened, the more I can help.'

At this Bonyfingers stopped moaning and rocking.

Her voice was frail, not the grand one she used with us. 'You must understand something, Dr Shaw. I rescued Mimi from a life of torment. She was owned by a family…a bad, cruel family. The parents let the children, well, not to put too fine a point on it…they let the children abuse her. I found it out from a neighbour. They teased her unmercifully. They

107

poked her with things – sharp pencils. They thought it was fun to watch her trapped in her cage while they made her suffer. And there was worse…but suffice to say, that's why she hates…hated…children. And another thing, Dr Shaw. Let there be no mistake on this. I had to go out for a short while but before I went I categorically told George not to go into the shed where I'd locked Mimi while we cleaned her cage. He disobeyed me, for all I know, spurred on by' – here she dropped her voice to a whisper – 'that Logan. An impossible child.'

My cheeks burned hot – hearing it said like that. *Logan, The Impossible.* I'd planned it and triumphed in my plan, filling the 'Impossible' Slot – you could say – to perfection. And now it seemed such a hollow victory.

Dr Shaw sighed and got up. 'Well, we can only be glad Mimi didn't get George's eyes or this situation would be unthinkable. Now, as it's Sunday, the vet is closed, but I know him. I can try to…'

'Thank you,' Mrs Everett interrupted. 'But I'll bury her myself, in my own garden.'

'It's a little more complicated than that,' said Dr Shaw. 'Mimi broke George's skin and this means there is a danger of transmission of…well…not to put too fine a point on it…disease. Mimi will have to be checked over by a vet. The hospital will insist on it. So I suggest I take her to him now. I pass his house on my way home.'

Mrs Everett stroked the lifeless Mimi, hardly listening. 'Poor darling. You didn't know what you were doing. Forgive me.'

She looked up at Dr Shaw. 'Is the boy...will he be all right?'

Dr Shaw nodded. 'I hope so and even if he is infected, there are effective antibiotics for both psittacosis and salmonellosis...the two most likely culprits.'

He put his head on one side like a bird. 'Mrs Everett, had you noticed anything about Mimi...ruffled feathers, diarrhoea...difficulties with breathing...which would indicate that she was carrying something?'

Mrs Everett shook her head. 'No, not...really.'

She didn't sound that sure – in fact I'd have sworn she *had* noticed something. Dr Shaw let it pass.

'Then there's probably nothing to worry about, but she will have to be tested. And you, what will you do now?'

'I'll pack and leave, of course.'

Dr Shaw took out a roll of white gauze and a clear plastic bag.

Mrs Everett said, 'The boy, Paul, he's old enough. He can keep an eye on the other two until their father gets back from the hospital. And then, well, it's up to them. But I can't stay here.'

'Very well,' says Dr Shaw. 'Now, if you don't mind…'

He took Mimi from Mrs Everett's lap.

Gently — as Mrs Everett let her tears fall — he wrapped Mimi in white gauze and slipped her, like a bird mummy, into the plastic bag.

They came together towards the hall. I sat back on the step with Tiff in my lap. I didn't care if they knew I'd been eavesdropping.

Dr Shaw took out one of his cards, scribbled on the back and handed it to Bonyfingers.

'Here's the vet's number. Call him in a couple of days and he'll let you know the position. Of course, if the tests are negative, you can have Mimi back to bury her.'

He tousled my hair, said his goodbyes and left.

And now it was Bonyfingers and me alone — facing each other. She without her Mimi. Me *with* my living breathing talking Tiff.

She took a shuddery breath and asked what she had to ask. 'How did the cat get to be there, in the garden, at that moment?'

110

Tiff sat up on my lap and answered before
I could.

'I escaped from the Rescue Home...with
Logan's help.'

Mrs Everett blinked hard and then – to my shock
and astonishment – *she answered Tiff straight back.*

# Chapter 17

## SHARING A STEP WITH THE ENEMY

'Of course you must have escaped,' she said. 'Or you *couldn't* have been there.'

She blew her nose with a small white handkerchief. 'And of course that's why Logan ran off to Burton…to prove you hadn't been claimed by any owner and to get you out. I knew as much.'

She looked at me directly, not noticing I was gobsmacked. 'And I'm sorry I lied to you about that, Logan. It was wrong of me.'

I couldn't speak even if I'd wanted to. This woman, who I'd hated so much, could understand Tiff like I could. What did that mean?

Tiff didn't seem surprised about it at all. She asked simply, 'Why did you lie?'

Mrs E tucked her hankie into her sleeve and sat

down on the step, which meant Tiff and I had to move along to make room.

She scratched Tiff's throat and settled herself. 'Ah,' she said, 'I told Logan you'd been claimed to save her from longing for you. Longing for what you can't have is such a terribly painful thing. And while Mimi was in this house, there couldn't be a cat, there just couldn't be. Mimi hated cats…and dogs for that matter…even more than she hated children. You see, the horrid little brats she lived with before I rescued her used to let her out into their small living room and set their cat and dog on her. On one occasion the cat caught her and began to maul her before they laughingly brought a stop to it. Apparently – I was told all this by their neighbour – for them it was a game. When I took her away from them, I promised I'd never make her share a house with a cat or a dog again.'

I tutted, embarrassed on behalf of children who could do such things and bring all kids a bad name as a result.

Mrs E went on addressing Tiff directly. 'Before I had Mimi, I had several cats. None of them spoke as well as you, but I always understood them. It's only a matter of tuning yourself in. By the way, how did you and Logan arrange the escape from the Home?'

Between us, Tiff and I told her – up to where we each ran our different ways.

'But what happened after that?' I asked Tiff. 'I waited for ages at the statue in the square. You didn't come and then a policewoman found me and brought me home. Where were you?'

'I'm sorry,' said Tiff, 'I got sidetracked. Someone else needed my help. A little boy lost – quite lost. And then, to be perfectly honest, I fell asleep in the sun after an excellent lunch at the back of a most wasteful restaurant.'

I laughed. And so did Mrs E. You just couldn't help it with Tiff. It was the way she put things.

'But after that?' I wanted to know the rest. 'Where were you, why didn't you call me? Had you forgotten my number? Or had you never memorised it?'

Tiff looked embarrassed. 'No, I knew your number, but I got a bit sidetracked again. Besides, I did try once. I slipped into a shop and tried to use the phone on the counter. But I was interrupted just as you answered. And afterwards, well, it isn't exactly easy for a cat to tap someone on the shoulder and ask to borrow their mobile phone.'

The image of her trying to do that set us off again; Mrs E and I giggling, and Tiff laughing like a donkey's hee-haw.

Then Verity blared down at me from upstairs. 'Logan! Come up here this minute! Paul and I want a word!'

She was so commanding I put Tiff into Mrs E's lap and obeyed.

Upstairs, Vee and Paul were white-faced.

'What are you *doing*?' Verity was really cross. 'What are you thinking of? That woman's mangy bird attacked our brother. She's the enemy! And you're sitting with her on our stairs and laughing with her. Hee-hawing with her.'

I stifled a giggle. 'The hee-hawing is Tiff. That's how she laughs.'

'Don't be so stupid!' My usually adorable willow-wand of a sister was raging. 'Why do you do this? Why do you always make everything so complicated and precious? Paul says you didn't speak one word for days, making everyone sick with worry and thinking of sending you to a psychiatrist. And now that I find you talking and laughing with Bonyfingers and claiming a cat can hee-haw like a donkey, I'm beginning to think you do need a shrink! We want that woman out of this house. Not sitting on our stairs, in our hall, laughing with you!'

There were a lot of things I'd have liked to say in reply, like: *Well, if you hadn't left us to stay with Farah,*

116

*you'd have been here and maybe you'd have stopped George going in the shed, or maybe you'd have taken us out on our bikes and he wouldn't have been there to help clean Mimi's cage.*

I didn't waste my breath. Verity would never grasp that by not being where she should have been – with us – she'd had something to do with what had happened.

Instead, I walked out of her room without a word, planning to go back downstairs and do some more talking and laughing with 'the enemy'. *To spite Verity, if nothing else.*

# Chapter 18
## ♪ TIFF EXPLAINS MIMI'S ♫ BEHAVIOUR

Neither Tiff nor Mrs E were on the step where I'd left them. I couldn't find Tiff in the house and went looking outside, calling her.

A window opened upstairs – the window of Mrs Everett's bedroom, usually the spare room.

Tiff leant out. 'I'm here. Come up. I've discovered something.'

When I got up to the room, she explained she'd found there were poisonous fumes coming in through an air-brick in the blocked-up fireplace.

I was not that surprised.

Our house was so old and so badly maintained, it was virtually falling down. The boiler was prehistoric and situated in the utility room right below Mrs Everett's room. The flue went up through

119

the chimney breast. No doubt it was cracked and spewing out fumes that were then wafting in through the air-brick.

'Toxic stuff,' said Tiff.

Mrs Everett sat on the bed beside an open suitcase.

'You mean Mimi or even I could have died in the night from breathing in the fumes?'

Tiff sniffed round the air-brick. 'They may have made you feel strange, but I don't think they'd have killed you. Parrots, on the other hand' – they chanted it out together – *'have very sensitive respiratory systems!'*

My heart sank. This house, this house. Everything about it was dangerous. Poisonous fumes were quietly, invisibly, seeping into our lives, without anyone realising it. And the 'not realising' was the most frightening part.

Especially if it was actually a case of realising but not admitting it, because once you did, you'd have to do something about it.

Surely my mother, at least, must have known the boiler was too old to be safe? You only had to listen to it coughing and chugging to know that.

Mrs Everett got up and began to pack, as if she now had double the incentive to get out of the house.

She took clothes off hangers at speed. 'You do

realise what this means?' she said as she folded furiously. 'If your father thinks he can sue me for compensation, or something, for Mimi's attack on George, then by the same token I can charge him with toxic waste poisoning! I could have damage to my lungs by now, who knows, while Mimi could be dead!'

'She is dead,' I said. 'And not because of fumes but because she attacked my little brother.'

'You don't have to remind me.' Mrs E pressed her face into a dress she was folding and smeared it with fresh tears and mascara.

'But here's another thought,' said Tiff. 'It's possible the fumes were affecting Mimi and that's why she attacked George. A matter of disturbed chemistry, not malice.'

I glared at Tiff. *Whose side are you on?*

In another way, though, I was glad truths were coming out. At least that stopped them lurking where you couldn't tell what they were up to.

'Well, there you have it,' said Mrs E, her voice breaking up with emotion. 'I'm certain that's what happened. Mimi was being deranged by toxic fumes from your boiler. I'll be writing to your father about it, Logan, be sure of that.'

She gathered toiletries and cosmetics from the dressing table. She was shaky and knocked several over. Some rolled onto the floor and the lid of a hairspray aerosol cracked.

'Damn!' she cried. It was all too much for her. She sat on the bed and wept – wracking sobs you wouldn't think could come from such a thin body.

'You have a good cry,' said Tiff. 'You deserve one.'

I wondered if I should stroke her as you're supposed to do with crying people.

Instead I helped Tiff pick up her things...lotions, bottles, lipsticks, eyebrow pencils and little pots of bright eye shadow and rouge. So much make-up for such a little amount of face, I thought, as Tiff pulled away the rest of the cracked lid from the hairspray.

As she did so, she stiffened.

'Ah ha!' She gave the button a push and breathed in the scent of the spray.

'More toxic stuff, I'm afraid...toxic for birds and many animals. Truly poisonous.'

She dropped the can into the wastepaper bin and brushed her paws. 'Mrs Everett, I know you're upset but I have to tell you. Boiler fumes or not, crammed together in this room, every time you used that spray you'd have been quietly poisoning your parrot.'

At that moment a car crunched up the drive: a taxi bringing Dad back from the hospital.

Verity and Paul thundered downstairs, Verity calling

(already forgetting she'd been cross with me), 'Dad's back, Logie! Come on! He'll have news of George!'

Of course, she didn't know where I was – which was just as well, because if sharing a step with Bonyfingers was bad in Verity's book, she'd have had a fit if she found I was in Bonyfingers' room, trying to comfort her!

I waited till their thundering had passed and said, 'I'll have to go down, Mrs Everett.'

She was packing at speed again. I imagined she didn't want to face much more of my family.

Tiff whispered to me. 'I'll give her a hand. She's in such a state, she shouldn't be left alone.'

I nodded. But I couldn't leave quite yet. 'Mrs Everett...' I began. 'I'm really sorry for you that Mimi is dead. And I hope she didn't have a disease that she's given to George. And if she has, I really hope my father doesn't sue you or anything. Especially as what Mimi did to George is probably because of poisonous fumes. And you didn't know about the hairspray. And we...well...we didn't really know about the boiler.'

I trailed off because the most difficult part still had to be said.

'And another thing...' I made myself do this. 'I'm sorry I've been so...impossible. But now I know you better and know you understand Tiff… well…maybe when Mum's back, Tiff and I can come and visit you?'

She looked at me with tears filling her eyes again — but a lovely smile.

'Thank you, Logan. I'd like that very much. Your mother knows where I am. All you have to do is call.'

And she turned back to her packing.

# Chapter 19
## WE MANAGE A FESTIVE SPAGHETTI AND DAD STRINGS SOME SENTENCES TOGETHER

Away from Mrs Everett and her problems, I was as excited as Vee that Dad was back.

I ran downstairs, thinking *maybe the pecks weren't as bad as we thought. Maybe the parrot disease tests are already done and George is clear and come home?*

It was no to both.

Dad had come back because George was sedated and sleeping.

Vee said Mum had asked him to phone her immediately when he got back from the hospital. She was waiting whatever time of day or night it was.

He called her on the phone in the hall where we could all hear him and huddle round to be closer to her.

When Dad finished he passed on the good news: she was arriving at 6 am, at London Heathrow, on

Tuesday, the day after tomorrow.

We cheered and, looking relieved himself, he disappeared into his study.

Tiff came bounding down the stairs into the hall to tell me that Mrs E was ready to go, would like to put her bags in her car, collect Mimi's cage, speak to Dad and leave.

Vee darted me a mean look. 'Oh yes, what's she saying now?'

I wouldn't give my sister the chance to be more cynical.

'Nothing,' I said. 'But Mrs Everett's leaving, you know. She's packed and ready and I suggest we get out of the way so she can...go...without us watching her.'

We took ourselves into the kitchen with Tiff and closed the door. Paul looked out of the window and said, 'That parrot cage is still out there on the lawn. I'd better take it round to her car.'

'Leave it,' said Verity. 'Please, just leave it, Paul. Let her do it. Pull the blind down so we don't have to watch.'

Paul dropped the blind and sighed. 'I wonder if Dad could go to the police and get a charge against her for not keeping her pet under proper control. Or at least sue her for it,' he said.

'I hope he does,' said Verity.

'I hope he doesn't,' said Tiff.

'So do I hope he doesn't,' I said.

Ignoring Tiff and me, Paul continued. 'I mean, what was she doing with a parrot like that when her job is looking after children? She's sick to even think of it. She *should* be charged.'

'It may be that she is sick,' said Tiff. 'Though not in the way you mean.'

'Did you hear that?' I asked to deaf ears because they hadn't.

So I told them what I knew because I thought, if *I* had to, then why shouldn't *they* start facing up to a few truths too. I explained about Mimi hating children and cats – all because of what a family had done before Mrs Everett rescued her. I informed them about the poisonous fumes being given off by our old boiler. And about parrots having very sensitive respiratory systems. And that it was quite likely Mimi had been deranged by the fumes and that's why she attacked George. (Needless to say, I made no mention of the fumes given off by Mrs E's hairspray!)

'So there,' I said when I'd finished. 'Maybe we can be a bit forgiving.'

Tiff nodded fiercely.

'And anyway,' I said, '*she* may charge *us*. Sue us for

millions for the poisonous fumes and then Mum and Dad will go to prison because if one thing's for certain, they won't be able to *pay*.'

Paul and Vee could hardly believe what they were hearing. *Me virtually taking Bonyfingers' side.*

'Well,' said Paul, 'I see you've got your voice back, Logie.'

'With *a vengeance*,' said Verity.

Paul asked how I'd found out about the boiler fumes.

'I sniffed them out in a trice,' said Tiff.

Paul and Vee glared at her. They did not comprehend what she said but they could hear that the sounds she made weren't like any normal cat.

So I told them about the boiler flue passing through the chimney breast in Mrs E's room and Tiff smelling the fumes through the air-brick.

Vee tossed her golden hair and tapped her foot in the most sarcastic way. *'Tiff smelt the fumes and told Bonyfingers they were from the boiler, did she?'*

'Yes,' I said.

'Yes,' said Tiff.

'And Bonyfingers understood her?'

Another simple 'yes' from me and Tiff.

And then Vee did the thing I hate most. She twisted her finger round in a circle next to her temple as if to say 'you're crackers'.

Paul, perfect Paul, was not sarcastic. 'Oh Logie, you're so…funny…so dramatic. Anyway, if Tiff's such a friend to you and to us why would she tell Bonyfingers about the fumes and give her a reason to sue us? Surely she's on our side?'

'I am on your side,' Tiff chipped in. 'But…'

I interrupted. 'Tiff's on everyone's side. The side of what's really happening. Don't you get it?'

No, they didn't get it.

So Tiff poured oil on the troubled waters and changed the subject. 'Let's make supper. I'm starving. It's five o'clock and I haven't eaten all day.'

I repeated her words for Paul and Vee. At least, this time, they laughed. And the idea of food was a good one. We were all hungry.

'What can you make?' Vee said to me, leaning against the counter and smoothing her arched eyebrows.

I could see her composing herself – after all her angry outbreaks of the day – and stepping back into her 'Too-Pretty-And-Adorable-To-Do-Anything-Difficult' Slot.

'Or let's get take-aways. Chinese or pizza. There's a new place opened in Porter Street. I bet they do free delivery. Got any money to pay, Paul? Dad won't have.'

None of us had any money so I agreed to make spaghetti bolognese with tinned sauce.

Tiff offered to help. I opened tins. She went into the garden and came back with parsley. 'Oh, and let's fry up some onion and garlic and add it to that tinned stuff. You'll be surprised at how much better it'll taste.'

Dad now came in and joined us, first washing his hands at the sink. Of Mrs Everett, I wondered?

'Well, she's gone and that's for the best, I think,' he said, opening a beer and offering one to Paul. Then as Vee humped that it wasn't fair, he opened a bottle of wine and gave her half a glass mixed with water.

Tiff got up on her hind legs. 'We could do with a splash of that wine in our sauce, Mr Dempster.'

Dad froze. '*What did she say?*'

There was a definite twinkle in his eye.

I told him, and added, 'Tiff knows what she's talking about when it comes to cooking, Dad. Though I don't know where she learned. Where did you learn to cook, Tiff?'

Tiff shrugged and dropped to all fours. 'Oh, trial and error, you know. Trial and error. And, of course, when you love eating you take an interest.'

I translated her words exactly for the others.

It sent them into gales of laughter.

'You're nuts, Logie,' said Paul. 'But funny with it.'

It was a good sound – that laughter – even if I was the butt of the joke. I turned from the cooker, waving a wooden spoon, and laughed too, thinking…*when was the last time any of us had hung out in the kitchen, fugged up with cooking, and laughed together. Even if it was the laughter of relief because Mrs Everett, the jangly stranger, had gone, George was going to be OK and Mum was coming home.*

I gave the sauce a last stir. Dad tested the spaghetti, levering out one strand, blowing on it, slurping it down and said, '*Perfetto, mia cara. Proprio come li cucinerebbe un italiano!*'

Dad speaking *Italian*? Then I remembered, of course he did. He'd written a jagged opera-thing in Italian which we'd had to sit through in a concert hall in London the one and only time it was performed.

Quite different to blessing me and my spaghetti in it, though. This was just getting better and better.

Vee took out some plates, holding them as if they might bite her. Paul got cutlery.

Dad strained the spaghetti and tossed it with the sauce.

We sat and passed it round.

Tiff, standing on her back legs beside me, coughed politely.

'Can she, please?' I begged. 'Sit with us?'

Dad nodded OK.

I laid Tiff a place next to mine.

Vee tossed her hair. 'A cat is not a doll or a baby. A cat should not be sitting at table with us.'

I ignored her. So did Dad and Tiff. She jumped up and sat perfectly upright on her chair – paws either side of her plate.

'Thank you,' she said as I passed her the spaghetti. 'I am enjoying this.'

Dad cleared his throat and tapped his glass with a knife.

'No, Tiff, it's we who have to thank you. You saved George from we dare not think what. Children, a toast to Tiff.'

He clinked glasses with me, mine fizzy with orange.

Paul and Vee stared, astonished.

'Dad,' Paul said. 'Dad, you answered her. You answered the cat. Does that mean she *is* speaking and you *understand* her?'

Dad's eyes rolled. 'Uh...well.' He was clearly mystified himself and embarrassed. 'Well, if I answered her, then...uh...I must have done, yes.'

Vee wrinkled her perfect nose. 'Mad as hatters, you and Logie. Cats don't talk our language, Dad. They just don't. End of subject.'

'I do,' said Tiff. 'And as I explained to Logan, I can't help what I am – a most unusual cat with talents that far exceed those of any other member of my species.

May I help myself to more of this delicious spaghetti?'

'OK, Dad.' Vee challenged. 'What did she say then?'

'Uh…something about talents?' said Dad. 'She has talents and this delicious spaghetti…?'

'Very good, Dad!' I thumped the table. 'You're getting it. As Mrs Everett said, it's only a matter of tuning in. Anyway, you thought she spoke that day we took her to the Rescue Home, didn't you?'

He ate and talked with enthusiasm, waving his fork about. 'Yes. To be honest. I did think there were certain cadences in the noises she – I mean you, Tiff – were making. They had the clear patterns of human speech. But you know, when something is as unlikely as that, our brains refuse to let us consider it seriously. Brains reject the unlikely as a kind of defence mechanism. In the case of a talking cat, we don't hear because we don't dare to hear. We don't want to believe in the possibility because it might rock our lives. Force us to change how we perceive everything.

'Of course, that's what my music is about. Pushing listeners – through the patterns of notes and sounds – to hear beyond what they're used to hearing or expect to hear, and open their minds to the possibility of impossibility, I suppose you could say. As that's what I do all day, if anyone should be able to understand you, Tiff – it's me!'

'Exactly,' said Tiff, reaching for a paper napkin and patting her mouth. 'Couldn't have put it better myself.'

She continued to eat daintily while Vee, Paul and I stared, mouths open, at our father.

He'd been stringing words into finished sentences and then stringing finished sentences into finished paragraphs! He'd probably said more, in just that one outburst, than we'd ever heard him say in one go. And on top of that, what he'd been saying was *interesting*.

It struck me as I gawped at him: *Maybe all the terrible things that had happened since Mum left for Australia had been necessary. Necessary, if things in our house were going to start to change for the better?*

# Chapter 20
## THE FESTIVITY FADES AND TIFF WANTS TO EXPLORE

Anyway, for good or bad, the terrible things *had* happened.

One festive spaghetti and some finished sentences from Dad were not going to change that. And soon enough the conversation came round to George, hurt and sedated in a hospital – not just because of Mrs Everett's parrot – but because of *everything*.

The festive spirit began to fade.

Verity started on at Dad about suing Bonyfingers for keeping a dangerous pet.

Tiff had an opinion on that and to Paul and Vee's annoyance, Dad listened to her.

'I believe Mrs Everett should be left alone with her grief,' said Tiff. 'She intended no harm and Mimi's dead anyway. She can't attack anyone else.'

Dad nodded (clearly understanding Tiff more, the more he tuned in), and I translated for Paul and Vee.

'Don't worry, Tiff,' Dad said, still finishing his sentences. 'We won't be pursuing this. Mrs Everett apologised very sincerely and also made it clear she'd told George he must not go into the shed. George disobeyed her so I doubt we'd have much of a case. In addition, she said she had reason to believe there were noxious fumes escaping from our boiler flue which were seeping into her bedroom. We'll have to look into it but if she's right, well, I suppose she could sue us.'

'See,' I said quietly to Vee, who tossed her hair and turned away.

Our festive supper was over. The mood had changed and anyway Dad was going back to the hospital in case George woke and needed him.

He wasn't keen to leave us alone and wondered vaguely about calling our neighbours. (Another first for Dad, as he never spoke to the neighbours.) But Paul reminded him that, aged sixteen, it was perfectly legal to leave us with him, while Vee pouted that, aged fourteen (which she was) it was perfectly legal to leave us with her!

'And anyway,' I said, 'Tiff's here.'

'I'll take care of them all, Mr Dempster,' said Tiff, and she meant it, probably in more ways than we realised.

Dad gave way. What was happening to us was private. We all felt it. Neighbours needn't know our beloved George was in hospital because of…what? Each of us being too absorbed in ourselves to keep a proper eye on him.

We scraped our plates. Sat sipping our drinks. None of us wanting to start the clatter that clearing the dishes would bring.

Instead, phones started. First, it was the hospital. George had woken so Dad found his car keys and left at the double.

Paul's girlfriend called next – or rather the girl closest to being his girlfriend out of all the girls who longed to be. She wanted him to go over. He didn't like to say no, apparently. *It was only a short ride on his bike. He'd be back soon. Would we be all right without him? Would we promise not to tell Dad?*

Then Farah rang and Vee disappeared into her bedroom to relate the dramas of the day. Would she mention Tiff's part in it all, I wondered? Probably not, because she didn't like Tiff (no doubt because Tiff was getting more attention than she was!).

By now, Tiff was dozing on the floor under the table

so I started washing up.

She opened her eyes. 'Leave some for Verity. That girl gets away with too much.'

I enjoyed the idea of making Verity do something beneath her beauty and left most of the dishes in the sink.

I sat on the floor beside Tiff.

'What shall we do? You and me,' I said. 'Shall I show you my model theatre?'

Tiff stretched gracefully, yawned and said, 'No. I'd like to explore.'

'Explore what? We can't go out at this time of night.'

'No, no. Explore here...the house.'

'Not very exciting for me,' I said. 'I *know* the house. Inside out. And anyway I don't want you finding more toxic stuff – not before Mum gets back, at least!'

She did her double-eyed blink. 'I wonder if you do know the house, Logan. When, for example, did you last go into your father's study?'

'When I dripped blood on a manuscript. Years ago.'

'Well, there you are,' she said. 'It's high time you found out where your father is coming from.'

# Chapter 21
## INTO THE FORBIDDEN

So, like a guilty trespasser, into the forbidden room I went, Tiff leading the way.

My guilt didn't last.

Tiff made nosing around in my father's study feel justified.

Obedient to the sign on the door, the room was not disturbed.

It was so dusty, it felt as if it hadn't been cleaned for years. Except, that is, for the grand piano, a trumpet in a silk-lined case and his curious collection of percussion instruments – not just the glockenspiel types but drums and cymbals and a glass cabinet with strange-looking bells and clappers and shakers and African-looking gourds. Not a speck of dust on any of them.

Tiff sneezed and complained but it didn't stop her investigations.

There were two massive, worn armchairs and two huge log baskets on either side of the fireplace – one basket piled with logs and kindling and one full of newspapers folded back to the crossword puzzles. The fireplace itself was filled with ashes and half-burnt logs.

On a table in one corner there was an old gramophone and piles of records, as well as an expensive-looking CD player and speakers and a set of big professional-looking earphones. (Probably what he was wearing when I was screaming for help for George.)

Hundreds of CDs were stacked alphabetically by composer, like books on shelves. Filing cabinets, some drawers pulled open and left open, were filled with his hand–scribbled music scores – no doubt many unfinished or finished and performed once, then forgotten about by him as well as everyone else who'd heard them.

In his field of 'experimental music', my father was definitely not at the top. Nowhere near. In fact probably close to rock bottom. But he didn't mind. Or so he claimed. He often said he was not writing his music *to have it accepted*.

Mum minded though – that he wasn't successful – and she minded even more that he didn't mind. '*Why can't you be like...*' she'd say, and an argument would begin.

Dad hated this more than anything – being compared to other equally experimental but well-known composers.

When Mum started on at him (which she often did), there'd be rowing and door-slamming – making the house shake to its unstable foundations.

I now picked up one of the scores from a pile on the floor, blew it free of dust and propped it up on the piano.

'Here we are, Tiff,' I said. 'If you want to find out where my father's coming from, come and have a look at this.'

Tiff left off examining the percussion instruments and joined me on the piano stool. 'Can you play?' she asked.

I'd had piano lessons for almost five years but never practised enough, didn't think I was any good, didn't enjoy being bad at yet another thing and, after much begging and moaning, was eventually allowed to give them up.

I could read music, though, and sight-read quite well, if the left hand wasn't too hard.

I started on Dad's score. There were so few notes it wasn't that difficult. Left hand first, one simple D major chord. Play it twice staccato. Then once more as the minor chord, that is without the F being sharp. Followed by…yes…three whole bars of rests (silence) and nothing for the right hand to do except add three high sharp Ds at the start of the second bar. Plink plink plink. Then another D minor chord with the left hand. Followed by a right-hand mash of sounds, harsh and unkind like a lost camel barking in a dust storm: a high D, F and G sharps, repeated as semi-quavers eight times – then silence for two bars – then repeated another eight times.

'Enough,' said Tiff. 'Pick out the melody for goodness sake.'

Turning to her on the piano stool, I put on a Verity-type eye-rolling face. '*What* melody, Tiff? Dad doesn't write *melodies*. If the most beautiful melody *in the world* jumped up his nostrils, he'd deny it.'

I don't know why this was so funny. I didn't mean it to be. But it was and Tiff started her donkey hee-hawing, which set me off.

We laughed so much we fell off the piano stool and rolled around on the floor – again the laughter of relief, this time because the thing that held our family to ransom *had been said out loud*.

Eventually we laughed ourselves out, got up and faced Dad's score again.

'OK, you've made your point,' said Tiff, 'but there must be some kind of melodic theme, tune, pattern…something in here somewhere?'

She turned a page, pointed to a section where the bars were filled with more notes than silence. 'Try that.'

I played the section as best I could.

'Is that it?' asked Tiff.

I nodded, trying not to start laughing again.

'Then play it again and again until I say stop,' she said.

I did and she listened intently – head on one side, her eyes closed.

Then she said, 'That will do,' and asked me to move over.

'I think,' she said, lifting a paw as if waving to an adoring audience, '*the missing melody has just been found.*'

# Chapter 22
## DRAWING DOWN THE NOTES

Tiff began to play my father's music on my father's grand piano.

The hairs on my neck stood up.

It was like watching someone type with two fingers at incredible speed. Only it wasn't someone typing.

It was a large black cat playing the piano, using the sides of her paws like fingers and her nimble, supple, stretching claw pads to achieve the chords.

Forget me and my 'Impossible List'. Forget behaving badly in order to be thought impossible. *This* was being impossible because this was The Impossible Being – *doing* the impossible right before my eyes!

Where Dad had left his precious silences, Tiff

was adding notes. And anyone with ears could hear they were the right notes – the notes that belonged there.

The music filled the study with arcs and curves and sweeps and runs of heart-stopping sound.

'Well?' She turned to me when she'd done, looking extremely pleased.

'Amazing,' I said, surprised I could speak at all. 'Incredible. *You're* incredible!'

'No,' she said. 'It's your father, not me. I played what he has written. The notes I've added are there to be read like meaning between the lines. They're hovering, waiting to be brought in.' She sighed. 'I'd say he leaves them out on purpose, Logan – though who knows why – he's a very perverse man.'

'You can say that again,' I breathed.

The shock of what I'd seen and heard had made me cold and shivery.

I got the fire going with newspaper and kindling.

It was a strange feeling – making myself at home in a room that had always been a threat, keeping our father from us.

The fire took. I settled in Dad's armchair, thinking: *If Tiff is right, my father CAN write great music. So why didn't he? That was the mystery. Maybe, I thought, he blocks it out deliberately, like he blocks out his family because he doesn't know how to deal with the complexities?*

If this was true then he must be made to stop. He must be made to draw down the notes from wherever they were – hovering above his scores – like the angels of sound.

Tiff, meanwhile, had been rooting around and found another score she wanted to try.

As before, she asked me to play it to her – as much as I could. And again when she'd heard enough, she edged me off the piano stool and began to perform it her way, drawing down the missing notes she was so easily able to find.

I snuggled deep into Dad's chair and listened to her play. Giving myself up to the music, I had the feeling that its beauty was so big, if it had been let out of the room, it would have filled the whole world.

Closing my eyes, I saw the piece being performed by a full orchestra in a great concert hall. Dad was conducting, handsome as anything in white tie. Mum, with jewels glinting at her throat, was not strained and tired. She shone and glittered with love and pride.

I was there too, black-eyed, black-haired, pug-nosed and plain maybe, but alight with happiness, held high by the glory and triumph of my father's music – beautiful beyond compare.

And when the piece finished in my imaginings, the audience raised the roof with its standing ovation and yelling of bravos and...the bit I liked most...flowers rained down thick all over the stage...lush, velvety, first-night flowers.

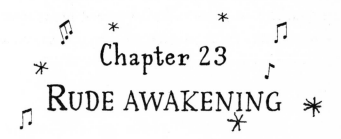

# Chapter 23
## RUDE AWAKENING

Some time later and I was being roughly shaken by Paul and Verity.

'Wake up, Logan!' Vee was shouting. 'What are you *doing* in here?'

'We heard the piano being played!' said Paul. 'What's going on?'

I struggled to sit up. To remember where I was.

It came back to me: Dad's study. Tiff playing his music with the missing notes returned. My dream of the concert and the first-night flowers.

I saw Tiff curled up on the piano stool.

She did her double-eyed blink. As if to say, 'Go for it. Let them know. Don't be afraid.'

'Well?' Verity paced on her willow-wand legs.

'Well, what?' I said, stretching slowly.

They were at a loss as to how to cope with me.

'We searched the house for you.' Verity was so inconvenienced it was funny. 'Then we heard the piano, and knowing it couldn't be Dad because he's at the hospital, we came to look in here. What are you doing, Logan?'

'Finding out where Dad is coming from,' I said coolly. 'About time one of us did, don't you think?'

I was smug, I admit it. High and mighty.

And so I should be. I had a cat who could not only talk and cook. She could play the piano like a prodigy, a virtuoso (words I knew from Dad). Like a complete and utter star!

'But no one comes in here, you know that,' said Paul.

I suddenly felt a hundred years old and that wise.

'Why?' I said. 'Ask yourself why. What is our father hiding from us?'

I got up and flounced Verity-style – to show her what it was like to be on the receiving end. Picked up some newspapers and threw them onto the fire. Flames and bits of fast-burning paper flew up the chimney.

'That he sits here doing crosswords and not composing? That when he *does* compose he composes mainly silence because he's scared to let in the notes he knows are there because he's scared of *his own talent?*'

Their white horrified faces stared at me.

I was not finished.

I flounced to the piano and picked up the scores Tiff had been playing from. I held them high as if they was going to follow the newspapers into the fire.

'No!' Vee gasped.

I tossed them back onto the pile of manuscripts on the floor and strutted to the door.

Tiff jumped off the stool and followed.

'And by the way,' I said, 'in case you were wondering *who* was playing that sublime music, I'll tell you.'

I paused for good effect.

Then uttered the one sweet word, 'Tiff.'

# Chapter 24
## TIFF COMES TO SCHOOL AND I GET IN WITH GERALD

Families! How do they get the way they get? For sure they don't start how they end up. Parents having their first child probably think...*what a strong ship we'll be.* We'll work like a good crew. Mother, father, kids. Together we'll sail the stormy seas of life. Hold fast against whatever the weather. Never let anything break us up, tear us apart. But then it doesn't work out like that.

It was the next morning. I was thinking these thoughts as Tiff and I got ourselves breakfast.

No sign of Verity and Paul although it was eight o'clock on a school Monday morning.

Maybe they'd decided they weren't going to school. I hadn't felt like it either but Tiff had persuaded me I'd feel better if I stuck to my normal routine.

'Time will pass faster,' she said, 'while waiting for news of George.'

She was eating a tin of sardines she'd decanted onto a blue plate – without any cutlery but as delicately as could be. 'When your world is upside down,' she said between mouthfuls, 'cling to the normal as hard as you can.'

I ate two bowls of cornflakes (not normal). I was starving and energised. Suddenly I *felt* like going to school (not normal). I didn't even feel guilty (not normal) that I was strong and happy while George was lying in a hospital bed.

Over the crunching cereal noises I was making, Tiff asked, 'Would you like me to come to school with you?'

'I would,' I said, 'but how?'

Tiff had ideas on this, of course. She would follow the school bus on foot and when we got to school, she'd meet me at an agreed place at an agreed time. 'I'll just be *a* cat – not *your* cat – sitting on a wall.'

We agreed she'd be on the wall at the top of the playground in first break.

'I'll introduce you to Cammy – my once-best friend,' I said.

'Good. I'd like to meet her.'

We were about to leave when Dad's car crunched

up the drive. He came in, slamming the kitchen door and joined us.

'How is he?' I asked.

'Not bad at all.' He switched on the kettle. 'They'll get the results of his tests and the tests on Mimi today and, if they're all clear, he'll come home as soon as your mother is back.'

'Tomorrow then!' Yippee. Beloved George.

Dad made a cup of tea and excused himself with a grunt.

It was as if the festivity at the spaghetti supper last night had never been. He was shutting off again. So not the moment to talk about Tiff drawing down the missing notes – in his own scores – to make the most beautiful music in the world only *he* didn't want to hear.

Tiff and I left for school and were turning the corner into the road when there he was. Half-running after us, down the drive, calling my name.

We stopped. He caught up. His face was red, his eyes popping.

*Stupid me*, I thought. *Why did I think he wouldn't notice someone had been in his study?* The minute he'd gone in he'd have seen that his precious scores had been moved, percussion instruments fingered, a fire lit, crosswords burnt.

Why hadn't I crept in there early and tried to hide the evidence?

He was so angry, he was trembling.

'*Everything's been touched!*' he exploded.

Getting down to my level, he took my shoulders. '*Who's been in my study? Was it you, Logan? It was, wasn't it?*'

I saw he was strangely terrified. This great big man, who could terrify us, was himself terrified. What was he hiding that made him so afraid of its discovery?

I said nothing, just meeting his eyes dead on. Then I pulled my shoulders free and stepped away as the bus chugged into earshot.

Perfect timing.

Thank you, bus. Thank you, Mr Marchant, the most impatient school bus driver ever.

'Here's the bus, Dad. I have to go. Mr Marchant *never* waits.'

I ran towards the bus stop. Tiff bounded after me.

We arrived as Mr Marchant was about to close the doors.

Tiff took a flying leap through them, nearly landing in his lap.

'Your cat can't come to school, Logan.'

'Just this once, Mr Marchant. Please? It's important.'

He adjusted his mirror, viewing the children behind

him, cleared his throat and addressed his passengers backwards.

'No one saw no cat on this bus. You all got it?'

No one got it. There were excited murmurs. Everyone strained over their seats to see the cat that wasn't supposed to be on the bus.

'Thanks, Mr Marchant.'

He whistled, looking ahead.

We sauntered down the aisle, Tiff and I. Everyone watching. For once, me cool as cool.

And then I saw Gerald.

Sitting at the back, the spare seat beside him taken only by his bag.

I went up and stood there till he moved the bag.

Tiff jumped onto the empty seat behind us.

I settled myself beside the Boy Genius.

He smiled at me. I smiled back.

He swivelled his neck round to look at Tiff, raised his eyebrows and smiled again.

Through the window – beyond Gerald – there was a view of my mad father. Frothing. Furious. Pressing himself back against the stone wall on the verge.

I saw Tiff waving at him.

Gerald saw it too.

We went a short way then he sighed and faced me.

He jerked his head, indicating Tiff behind us, and

dropped his voice. 'Your cat. It waved at that man on the side of the road.'

'Yes. She knows him. He's my dad.'

Gerald rubbed his chin. 'That's not what I'm saying. Cats don't wave. Not the way she did. Like the Queen.'

I scanned his face. This boy. I liked him so much.

He meant everything to me. He meant lights that really work and curtains that open and close at the push of a button. Gerald, the electronics wizard. The one-day great scientist who already knew how to make a cathode ray and a silicon chip. Coolest boy in the class, the school, the world, the universe.

Chances come and chances easily slip by if you don't take them.

I wriggled down deep in my seat. Pulled my scarf up so my mouth was partly hidden and tempted him in a thick scarfy conspiratorial voice.

'If you really want to know, Gerald…'

He did and he leant so close to hear me our hair touched. 'She doesn't only wave like that. Like the Queen. She talks. As well as or better than we do. *And* she plays the piano like *a virtuoso.*'

It was at this moment that I began to love Gerald and not just like and admire him. For this reason: I could see he didn't doubt me. Not for a second.

He was perfectly fine with *believing* me.

All he wanted was more and I offered it.

'If you like, and if you promise not to say anything to anyone, I'll let you hear her talk for yourself in first break.'

# Chapter 25

# TIFF PLAYS FOR GERALD AND I'M A CHILD PRODIGY

At school, we sorted out our stuff and filed to assembly – though not as usual. That morning it was Gerald and me – *walking together.*

It was noticed immediately because usually Gerald never walked with anyone to assembly.

Cammy's eyes were popping and so were Clarky's.

In assembly, he was my bodyguard. Continually checking round like I was the prime minister and as if to say: *Look at her wrong? And you're dead.*

Lessons flew by. My back was straight. I was listening and for once hearing what I was listening to.

Always I could see Gerald, two rows over to my left. Two desks in front.

He kept looking back to check I was still there. As if afraid I'd disappear before I'd introduced

161

him to the unnatural wonders of my talking cat.

Once he smiled and winked at me.

Cammy, sitting at my side, saw and passed me a note.

I didn't have to open it to know what it would say and it did: *Guess who's got a crush on u. Gerald the Genus.*

I added the 'i' to genus and passed it back.

Smug I was, so smug.

The first-break bell rang. Now, of course, because Gerald was interested in me, Cammy wanted to be connected to me by the hip. The one break that I didn't need her. I said I couldn't. That I had 'stuff' to do. Knowing I'd be made to regret it in due course.

Outside, the playground was heaving with running, screaming, tagging, kicking kids – too absorbed in letting off steam to pay attention to us.

Gerald and I walked unnoticed over to the top wall.

Tiff was there. Hunkered down, her big yellow eyes copping everything, missing nothing.

As we approached she sprang off the wall and streaked down the narrow passage between the playground boundary and Form 4 classroom.

The passage – filled with weeds and some builders' rubble – was 'out of bounds'. I beckoned to Gerald and we followed.

Tiff was at the end of the alley, perched on an upturned plastic bucket. There was just enough room for Gerald and me to crouch down beside her, shoulder to shoulder.

'Tiff, this is Gerald.'

Tiff put out a paw, coy, delicate. 'Hello, Gerald.'

Gerald didn't hesitate to shake the paw.

'I thought it was Cammy I was to meet,' said Tiff. 'Your once-best friend.'

'I heard something!' Gerald's cheeks reddened. 'I'm sure I did! I heard...best friend.'

'Good! Tune in and you'll hear it all. Ask her a question.'

He took a breath. 'Uh...Logan says you play the piano. Is that true?'

Again Tiff gave him her coy look. 'I do, yes. Unusually for a cat and rather well at that.'

Gerald spluttered. 'I heard quite a lot there. Unusually...for a cat...rather well!'

'You'll be tuned in before you know it,' I said, proud of him.

'Oh, I do like you, Gerald,' Tiff now flirted. 'I like you a lot.'

Gerald laughed. 'Heard that all right. Not sure how it's happening but it is...even if there isn't a scientific explanation.'

'Does there have to be? I mean, always, a scientific explanation?'

He shook his head. 'No, it's just that there usually is. I wonder. I wonder if...well, could I hear you play the piano? That is if you wouldn't mind?'

Tiff double-winked. 'But where?'

Gerald suggested the piano in the school hall. No one was allowed in the hall at break unless it was raining. But Gerald said he thought we could sneak in without anyone noticing and Tiff could play for him there. If anyone heard they'd most likely think it was a teacher and walk on by.

We sent Tiff the long way round so she didn't have to cross the playground. Gerald and I slipped in separately – him first, me a bit later.

The hall was empty except for the piano and some gym mats that hadn't been put away.

Gerald opened the piano and Tiff jumped onto the piano stool.

It was too low for her to reach the keys comfortably, so she stood on the seat, positioned her paws above the keys, and closed her eyes.

'What shall I play? I think the second of your father's pieces. I like that one.'

Opening her eyes, she began – letting the angels of sound dance for Gerald.

His face was a picture – of shock and amazement.

He spread his hands and hunched his shoulders as if to ask, *how can this be?*

I shrugged shyly. The marvel of it was not my doing. I couldn't take the credit.

We heard the high heels advancing before we saw Miss Notts, the Head, coming towards us.

Keeping his cool, Gerald pushed me onto the piano stool. Tiff, getting the message, jumped off and slipped round the side of the piano.

By the time Miss Notts was close enough, it looked as if it was me who'd been playing.

Good in a way. Not in other ways.

'Logan!' she cried out in surprise. 'I didn't know you could play so beautifully.'

A hot blush spread across my face.

'Does Mr Crow know about this?' (Mr Crow was the music and drama teacher.) I shook my head – praying Gerald would think of something to make the situation go away.

'Well, he ought to know about it.' She scratched behind an ear. 'He must hear you, Logan. A child prodigy in our school. Goodness. Make the Ofsted lot sit up. But then again…' She walked round in a circle thinking aloud, her heels clipping. 'Maybe not so surprising. Your father is a composer, isn't he?'

Dread seeped through me as I nodded, knowing what was coming next.

'Well, I must talk to him about you. I'll phone him after school.'

'I wouldn't,' I stammered. 'He doesn't like to be disturbed. Ever. He works all the time.'

Miss Notts ignored that. She was on to the next thing. 'Of course, I'm aware you're not supposed to be in here, either of you. But given what I've just heard, I'll overlook it. Now, off you go and play outside.'

Jumping off the stool, I thought we were out of trouble. We weren't.

'By the way, what were you playing?'

Gerald answered for me, not having the faintest idea it was the last thing I wanted him to say. 'One of her father's compositions. It's a brilliant piece.'

'I agree.' Miss Notts considered for a second. 'I was listening from the corridor. Extraordinarily beautiful.'

Then, 'You know, Logan, I think I'd like Mr Crow to hear you play right now. I'll see if he's in the staff room.'

Tiff came to my rescue.

She appeared from round the side of the piano, arched her back, hissed and jumped onto the keyboard.

Miss Notts cried, 'Oh my God, what's a cat doing in here?'

Whereupon Tiff started walking up and down on the keys, swishing her tail and creating a mishmash of the ugliest sounds.

Miss Notts tried to shoo her off, which Tiff was not having, of course.

Now it was Gerald to the rescue, 'Better get the caretaker, Miss Notts! A cat like this could be dangerous. Looks right feral – probably from the woods. Come on, Logan, we'll run for Mr Bristock!'

We tore out of the hall.

Tiff followed, shooting past us. As she went she said, 'Meet you at the gates after school.'

And she was gone – streaking round the edge of the playground and under the locked gate, making for the scrubby grassland behind the school.

Gerald and I melted into the first-break crowd – relieved and panting.

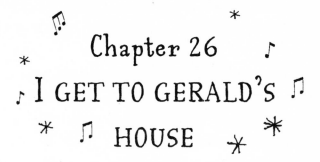

# Chapter 26
## I GET TO GERALD'S HOUSE

For the rest of the school day, I focused on not being summoned to play for Mr Crow.

I considered telling our teacher I felt faint and would have to go home. Gerald pointed out that I shouldn't. If I was sick someone would have to fetch me. If my father came, Miss Notts would have the chance to tell him I was a child prodigy and then I might have to play for *him*.

Best thing for me to do, Gerald thought, was to *lie low*.

Keep out of Miss Notts' sight. If she did summon me, tell her the truth.

'Say it wasn't you playing but the feral cat.'

'But she'll say I'm a liar.'

'No,' said Gerald. 'Because she could never believe

in a cat playing the piano and she knows she heard *someone* playing, so she'll construe that you're too shy to play for Mr Crow. Kids being shy is fine by school heads. She'll be comfortable with that. She won't push you.'

No question about it. Gerald was a genius who had the way grown-ups think sewn up.

As it happened, Miss Notts did not send for me to perform. The school day ended with no further excitement except for kids who'd been on the bus that morning asking me where my cat was.

Cammy and Clarky watched as Gerald and me walked down to the gates together.

They followed a few steps behind, giggling hysterically.

Tiff was tucked under a straggly bush a few metres from the bus stop.

We went up to her, kicking at loose stones on the road side as if we hadn't seen her.

I pretended to tie a shoelace. 'There you are, Tiff. Are you OK? Did you find stuff to do?'

'Lots. I like it round here.'

Gerald crouched beside me. Skimming a loose stone.

'I have an idea,' he said. 'Why don't you come home with me for tea. Both of you?'

I think I glowed so hard I must have resembled

a light bulb – just switched on.

Tiff rubbed her face with a paw and yawned. 'You go, Logan. I'll be honest. I'm people-pooped for today. I need to be by my catlike self. And those woods are calling.'

She promised to be back at our house by eight o'clock exactly.

So now it was just us – Gerald and me. Walking up Harebell Hill to his house. I wondered as we walked and asked, 'If you live here, so close to school, why were you on the bus this morning?'

'Spent the weekend in Ragden.' He said it in a way that meant *just leave it*.

Round the last bend we arrived at a white cottage covered in large once-purple flowers now fading to mauve and losing their petals.

How cool it must be, I thought, to live five minutes' walk from your school. Instead of a forty-minute bus ride. Tumble out of bed of a morning, into your school kit, a few minutes before school starts. Eat your toast as you walk down the hill.

Everything about Gerald was like this: the best.

As we went into the house, through the kitchen door, he called out to his mother that he'd brought a friend home.

His mother called back, 'Hello, darling. Hello,

friend. I'll join you shortly.'

'She's probably working.' He threw down his bag and struggled out of his blazer. 'What shall we eat? I'm starving.'

'Me too,' I admitted.

The kitchen was fantastic. A bright primrose room. A warm orange cooker. Big scrubbed table and a hodgepodge of wicker chairs filled with cushions, each chair large enough for three cats to sleep in comfortably.

Vases of flowers, dropping petals on the window sills, books piled everywhere. Two vast canvas paintings on the walls – one of vividly coloured, cubed women, the other of red peppers and a red jug over an intensely blue background.

'Great room,' I said.

'Yeah. It's good.' He was busy sorting through a basket of vegetables.

'Baked potatoes with runny egg and cheese?'

'Sounds great.'

He clattered about, at home, cooking for us – scrubbing the potatoes, putting them in the microwave, slamming the door, setting the dials, whistling – like he did this every day.

I felt a bit awkward, standing there with nothing to do but watch him.

He called out to his mother as he ferreted in the fridge, telling her what he was making and asking if she would like some.

She called back that she'd have a little.

He cracked eggs into a white bowl.

'My mother's a painter.' He lowered his voice. 'Eats like a bird. Drinks like a fish.' He laughed.

I blushed for him – that he had such a thing in his life to mention.

'Actually…' He paused in his egg beating. 'That is nonsense. Fish don't drink. So a bad metaphor. What would be a better one. What drinks a lot?'

'A camel,' I offered.

'Better. Drinks like a camel. And she can hold it too – like a camel.'

More blushing from me. He didn't seem embarrassed.

He went into the garden to get some chives.

I turned on my phone. A text bleep announced a message from Cammy and no prizes for guessing what it said: *do u fancy boy genus lol c.*

Horrified he'd sense it on the airwaves, I snapped off the phone just as he returned.

'Anything interesting?' he asked.

'Only Cammy being silly.'

'Most girls are silly,' he said, sharing another of his

theories. 'I wonder why? Must be biological.'

He chopped away at his chives.

'In other words, they have to be, to make boys feel they're more serious and therefore superior. Maybe that's it. Though you're not silly. Except sometimes when you're trying to keep up with Cammy – I mean keep up with her silliness. I have noticed that.'

He'd noticed. I couldn't believe it. And he didn't think I was silly when I wasn't around silly Cammy. Could a day get better?

It could and it did.

What he'd just said gave me the confidence to tell him about my model theatre. About my idea to have lights that actually worked and maybe curtains that drew *electronically*. I asked him if he'd be interested in working on it.

It was that easy. *He'd love to*, he said. *And while we were about it why didn't we put on a show in the theatre? Had I thought of that? Had I thought of animatronic puppets?*

Before I could ask what animatronic puppets might be, his mother came in.

She was wearing a baggy white shirt covered in paint. There was paint in her mop of red hair and a splodge of white on her cheek. Completely beautiful – to my eyes anyway. Her red mouth beamed.

Gerald introduced us. 'Mum, this is Logan and Logan, this is my mum, Greta.'

Greta held out a hand covered in paint, then seeing the paint laughed, withdrew it and gave me a light kiss on the cheek instead. 'At least that's paint-free.'

She cleaned her hands with kitchen towel and white spirit. Gerald said it stunk and she shouldn't do it in the kitchen.

I loved the smell of the white spirit mixed with oil paint.

She asked Gerald if he'd had a good weekend.

He had, he said.

With her hands clean she went to the fridge, took out a bottle of wine and poured herself a glass.

She settled opposite me at the table – fished out a packet of cigarettes and lighter from a pocket and lit up.

All the time talking. She asked me everything, where I lived, if I had brothers and sisters, what my parents did.

'Do you know,' she said, 'I've heard of your father. In fact I have a CD of his. I'll look it out in a minute. In certain moods it's great to paint to. It's all so non-modular, his music, that it kind of bypasses this side of the brain.' (She grabbed the left side of her mop of hair.) 'And rouses this side.' (She grabbed the right side.) 'Very useful when you want to access images you know are lurking but haven't quite got hold of, if that makes sense. Probably not, but anyway I find it very stimulating – your father's music. It's so bravely experimental it makes *me* brave and experimental. Tell him I said so. Thank him for me.'

I said, 'My little brother calls his music "mental music".'

This made her give a great roar of laughter. White teeth flashed behind the startling red lips. I loved being able to make her laugh. Though mentioning George brought a stab of worry.

I pushed it away. George was going to be all right. Nothing must be allowed to spoil this.

Greta refilled her glass.

Gerald brought carrot juice for him and me – it looked great and tasted disgusting.

Still, I was glad to find out what he liked. Maybe stuff like carrot juice made him the genius he was.

Next, he brought huge white plates of food.

This was not disgusting. The opposite.

Greta ate three teaspoons of runny egg and a few chives.

Gerald asked if he could tell his mother about...

I thought he was going to say Tiff, which I wouldn't

have been happy with. Tiff was becoming too public for comfort.

But it wasn't Tiff – thank goodness – it was my model theatre.

I said sure.

Greta got very excited, especially about the idea of staging a show. She'd help design the sets, she said.

Gerald raised his eyes at me as if to say, *we're not letting her near it.*

She suggested my father could provide the music.

This fired Gerald up. *Perhaps we could put on a musical or a small opera? And the more ambitious it was, the more electronics we'd need. Revolving sets maybe. Why not? It would be such fun.*

'But,' he said, 'there is a bit of a problem. I'll have to work on the theatre here at this house because I've got all my equipment here.'

I said he could bring the theatre over but wondered how. 'It would be difficult to bring on the bus.'

'Hmm,' said Gerald, smiling at me and reaching for his mother's glass of wine to put it back in the fridge. 'Mum, any chance you'd take us over to Logan's to fetch it? Like, now? I can't wait to take a look at the thing.'

Greta mock-groaned. 'You kids. Oh, why not? It's not too far, is it?'

We finished eating and drove to my house.

I pinched myself all the way.

Gerald the Boy Genius was coming to my house because he couldn't wait to get his hands on my theatre and *make the lights work*.

# Chapter 27
## BAD NEWS FROM AUSTRALIA AND GRETA SMOOTHES OUT DAD

As we went in at the front door, Paul and Verity rushed down the stairs yelling at me, not realising I wasn't alone.

'Logie! Where have you been? Your phone was off...' They saw Gerald and Greta and pulled themselves up.

I introduced them and added, 'I've been to their house for tea. Gerald's going to help with my theatre.'

Paul and Vee shuffled nervously.

Clearly something was going on they didn't want to speak about in front of strangers.

Greta picked up on it right away.

'Look, if this is a bad moment, we can get the theatre another time.'

'Or now,' said Gerald, 'and just go.'

Verity started crying and blurted it out. 'Mum phoned! Grandad has died!'

'So she can't come back tomorrow,' said Paul more calmly, 'and she wants Vee and me to go over for the funeral to support her. You're to stay here with Dad and George.'

Vee sat on the stairs and sobbed. Greta, who didn't know us, took charge.

She took us into the kitchen and put on the kettle.

She asked quiet questions until she'd heard the full story from the moment Grandad tripped over the paving stone to George being attacked by Mrs Everett's parrot and going to hospital.

She was a bit shaken by that and turned away as if *she* was about to burst into tears. 'Goodness, what a time you've all had. I'm so sorry. So very sorry.'

This, of course, only made Vee cry harder – because that's what a lot of sympathy does to you. For a bit there was silence between us except for Vee's crying and Greta rattling cups and spoons.

Then she placed a large mug of camomile tea in front of Vee saying, 'There, sweetheart. You drink that. It'll calm you. Anyone else for a cup?'

We shook our heads and she sat down at the table and asked where Dad was.

Paul said he was at the hospital and that he didn't yet know about Grandad because you have to turn your phone off in hospitals and they hadn't got hold of him.

'Did you know your grandfather well?' Greta asked.

We said no.

'Well, that's one small blessing because it means you won't miss him too much. And George? How is George? He is going to be all right, isn't he?'

Paul told us he'd seen him that morning and he was fine and cheerful too. The tests on Mimi had come back negative and he was hopefully coming home tomorrow.

'I see,' said Greta, moving on smoothly the way she did in order to get the whole picture. 'So when will you and Verity be going to Australia?'

'Mum wants us to go as soon as we can get on a flight,' said Paul. 'I'm looking on the internet to see what flights there are.'

'Good,' said Greta. 'And what are you going to take to wear, Verity? The climate is the other way round in Australia. It's spring over there.'

I wondered how Greta knew that the best way to get Vee's mind off sadness was to get it onto clothes.

She cheered up at once. 'Oh great, then it'll be

shorts and strappies. Except for the funeral. I've never been to a funeral. What'll I wear?'

She went upstairs to hunt through her wardrobe and find something suitable.

Paul went to continue hunting for flights on the internet.

Left with Gerald and me, Greta smiled. 'Why don't you two go and look at your theatre, Logan. I'll take a walk round your wonderful garden. I don't want to leave you before your father gets back.'

Gerald and I went upstairs. As I was about to open my bedroom door, it dawned on me. *The room was still the tip I'd artificially made it while being impossible!* What with George being attacked by Mimi and the rest, I hadn't had a moment to tidy up.

My cheeks burned. How could I let Gerald see the pigsty it would seem I was happy to live in?

And then a worse realisation: my List of Things To Do To Be Impossible was still stuck on my wall – with all its big fat red ticks. So childish. So totally totally cringe-makingly uncool.

He stood beside me waiting for me to turn the handle and open the door. And must have read my thoughts.

'You should see *my* room. Anyway, they say it's a sign of genius – being able to function in a mess.

They say over-tidy people are just, you know, a bit…retentive. While mess is organic. You grow more in it.'

I smiled and opened the door, crossed the room and whipped the cover off the theatre. Then while – to my joy – he went, 'Wow! this is going to be good!' I ripped The List off the wall and slipped it into a drawer. He wasn't going to see *that*, not if I could help it. Why? Because that was then. This was now: Logan Dempster in the middle of a world with Tiff and Gerald in it. A world where everything was *possible*.

And to that end, we were soon carried away thinking about all the things we could do to the theatre and what kind of show we'd put on.

I didn't tell him about my, 'Mr and Mrs Dumpster and Verisimilitude Dumpster' play. Far too close to home.

Anyway, Gerald had all sorts of ideas about how we could really stretch ourselves *technically* – by putting on something full of action like Hannibal and his wars with Rome.

'Or the Carthaginians' war with their own mercenaries, who they couldn't afford to pay so they fought them instead! I've been reading about that though it's not a hundred per cent known if it's truth

183

or fiction. Not that it matters. We could have animatronic boats sailing about with moving waves and crashing music,' he declared, completely thrilled at the idea. 'And horses and armoured elephants and stuff like that.'

We were so carried away with the possibilities in my *geniusly, organic, untidy room*, I didn't hear Dad coming home.

Eventually he came to find us. 'Good to meet you, Gerald. I've been talking with your mother. But she'd like to go now so you'd better get that...uh...that theatre...into her car.'

Gerald lugged it downstairs and put it on the back seat. I followed and watched as Dad and Greta approached from the house, over the gravel, deep in conversation.

Greta had a handful of CDs – obviously more of Dad's non-modular music to paint to. She waved them about as she talked.

At the car, Dad shook her hand.

'Thank you, thank you so much for staying...'

'A pleasure.' She flashed her white teeth. 'Glad to be of a little help, even if it was by accident. Now don't forget, anything I can do in the next few days, just call. And as I said, Logan is more than welcome to stay with us.'

'Thanks,' said my father. 'But if I can persuade the hospital to let George come home, I'm going to need Logie here.'

Greta climbed into the car and wound down the window.

'Thanks for the CDs, Howard.' She started up the engine.

Dad bowed, smiling – looking happy and handsome, smoothed out and sure of himself. It was as if Greta had given him a steam iron, uncrumpling the creases of his awkwardness completely.

'See you tomorrow,' said Gerald, getting in the back with the theatre. He lowered his voice. 'And say hello to Tiff for me.'

He put his arm over the theatre as if it was a precious possession.

Their car disappeared down the drive, leaving me walking on air.

There was a lot to face up to, of course. Dad was bound to get back to the business of who had been in his study last night. And then there was the possibility of Miss Notts ringing to tell him I played the piano like a child prodigy.

But the great thing was: I didn't care.

Not now that Gerald (Coolest Boy In The Universe) – who could make lights work, sets revolve,

185

theatrical boats sail in theatrical seas – had moved to centre stage in my life.

I was like a helium balloon someone had just let go.

All the stuff that usually kept me miserably stuck on the ground had been left far below.

Soon, when I got upstairs, I would take The Impossible List out of the drawer, tear it into a million pieces and throw them like confetti to the breezes of history.

And flying this high, I felt I could handle anything. Even Grandad dying. (Well, I had hardly known him at all, to be fair.) Even Mum not coming home tomorrow and certainly anything Dad could throw at me.

# Chapter 28
## DAD UNCRUMPLED DOING THE UNTHINKABLE

So what *had* Greta done to Dad in just a few hours?

Praised him to the skies? Told him his music was brilliant and that it unlocked her painting brain?

Whatever it was, in those few hours he'd spent talking to Greta, he'd changed.

He put his arm round my shoulders, smoothly, not in his usual clumsy, should–I–shouldn't–I way, and walked me towards the house.

'What a lovely woman,' he sighed. 'She's very concerned about us. And, Logie, I'm so sorry about your grandad and about your mother having to stay on in Australia. I really am. And Paul and Verity going off. But we'll be all right here, for another week or so, won't we?'

Well, I certainly would! I had Tiff and I had Gerald.

187

'Nice boy too, that Gerald,' said Dad.

'He's a genius. I mean really one. At science and electronics and stuff.'

Dad chuckled.

'And you…you and I have a lot to talk about. Not only do you have to explain what you were doing in my study, you also have to explain how you've become a child prodigy at the piano overnight.'

I stole a quick look at him. His eyes were twinkling. There was not a trace left of the flaming rage he'd been in that morning. It was going to be OK, I figured, thanks to Greta. Maybe all I had to do was tell him the truth?

'So,' Dad stopped at the front door. 'Let's start with Miss Notts. She called while I was talking to Greta. She was very excited about you. Said you have a major talent. She wants to arrange a concert to show off your skills. Now, the thing is, and no offence meant, Logie, but you and I know you can hardly get through 'Autumn Leaves' without a mistake. So who *was* playing there in the school hall? It wasn't Gerald because I asked Greta and she told me he can't play at all. So? What was going on?'

I didn't answer as we went into the hall.

His DO NOT DISTURB sign was crooked on the door. He saw me looking at it.

In the next instalment of doing the unthinkable, he now lifted the sign off its hook and said with a small, questioning smile, 'Are you going to come in and tell me what's going on?'

It really was unbelievable. I'd never been invited into his study. No one had – except his manager, Daniel, and musicians he worked with.

But now, here I was: invited to sit in the armchair opposite his. He threw a few logs onto the fire, poured himself a drink from a tray and made himself comfortable.

'Right. Begin at the beginning, Logie. It was you in here last night, wasn't it?'

I nodded.

'So, why?'

I figured he wasn't exactly going to take out a gun and *shoot* me whatever I said, so I said, 'Tiff wanted to explore. She said we should come in and find out where you were coming from. She said it was about time.'

Then, not wanting it to sound as if I couldn't decide things for myself, I added, 'Though it's not Tiff's fault. I wanted to.'

'I see. And what did you find?'

'A lot. All your instruments, and I saw you do a lot of crosswords.' He looked embarrassed at that. 'And then we looked at that pile of music there and…we tried some out.'

'*We* tried some out?' He frowned. 'We?'

'Tiff and me. The thing is, Dad…Tiff can…'

'Don't say it.' He drained his glass. 'A cat who can communicate is one thing, but please don't ask me to hear you say *she plays the piano*!'

'Well, she does.' I slipped it out as fast as I could.

He laughed the same big deep lovely laugh I'd heard in the Rescue Home car park.

Then, 'How old are you, Logie? Twelve? Thirteen? Surely you shouldn't still be living in fantasy land?'

That he didn't know how old his own daughter was irritated and hurt me.

'I'm twelve and you should know that. And I'm not living in fantasy land. Tiff plays the piano brilliantly. And, if you want to know the truth, *that's* who Miss Notts heard. Think about it. It wasn't Gerald. You know it couldn't have been me. But Miss Notts heard something amazing or she wouldn't have phoned you. *So who else could it have been?* There was no one else in the hall!'

I was on my feet shouting that last bit.

'Uh…some other child…or a recording…yes

a recording...some trick you and Gerald got up to.'

'Except it wasn't, Dad. I promise.'

He got out of his chair and paced about, fiddling with the trumpet in its open, silk-lined case.

He now left the impossibility (in his mind) of Tiff playing the piano and moved on to the next part of the mystery (as he obviously found it to be).

'Miss Notts said the piece being played was one of mine. Truly beautiful, she said. So which piece was that?'

I picked up the score we'd been 'messing with' from the top of the dusty pile and handed it to him.

He set it on the piano's music rack.

'That's odd. I never finished this. Lost interest in resolving the counterpart. Certainly wouldn't say it's "truly beautiful".'

I knew this was the moment to tell him about the missing notes that Tiff could hear and draw down to fill the silences.

Not an easy thing to explain to your composer-father when you are his twelve-year-old kid who is supposed to know zilch about music.

And right then, I didn't have to.

Dad's phone rang. It was Paul wanting to speak to him about the tickets to Melbourne.

And talk about my father doing the unthinkable.

I could hardly believe what I was hearing him say. 'Uh, Paul...Logie's with me in the study. Why don't you and Verity join us and we'll make our plans?'

# Chapter 29
## ROUND DAD'S FIRE

For any other family, normal. For ours, paranormal: Paul, Verity and Dad sitting round a licking fire in Dad's study talking about…well…just about everything.

It didn't happen immediately. First we were all a bit self-conscious: Verity and me exchanging secret looks, even easy-going Paul not quite sure what to do with himself — sit, stand, stretch his legs out towards the fire; be himself or be on his guard.

But, as Dad began to relax and stretch out, so did we.

And gradually the conversation went from the urgencies of the moment — George and Grandad and Mum — and the boring but necessary 'arrangements' like flights to Australia and check-in times and what you wear to funerals – to the bigger picture. The *interesting* picture of – I suppose you could say – how we came to be. Us, the Dempsters. As we were at that moment.

After some prompting from me (well, more like a direct question), Dad told us how he and Mum had met. It was at a mutual friend's party in Chelsea in London. Mum was at the Chelsea School of Nursing and Midwifery and Dad was at the Royal College of Music (so someone must have thought he'd had talent then or he'd never have got in there).

He said he knew he was going to marry her within ten minutes of meeting.

And they had married – almost the minute they'd both qualified – in Melbourne, Australia because that's where Mum was from and where her parents lived.

They'd lived there for two years before coming back to England, Mum working at the Melbourne General Hospital and Dad going off into the bush on his own (even then and even though they were newlyweds) to try to notate the sounds of the outback. And where one morning he stood on a Western Brown (a poisonous snake) and didn't die because it only bit him – as a warning – and didn't inject its venom.

'Though I could have died from sheer fear that I was going to die, alone in the outback with my new wife pregnant with our first child – you, Paul,' Dad chuckled.

We'd heard some of this from our mother over the years, but hearing Dad say it in his own way and words was, to my mind, more thrilling.

Then the road to the past curved round again to the present and how we lived now…only we kept off 'urgencies and arrangements' and talked about what bothered me so much. The crumbling house with its sloping floors, cracking walls and toxic boiler. And then – and it was Verity who brought it up, not me – the DO NOT DISTURB sign on Dad's study door.

'We hate it, you know, Dad,' she said, pouting her pretty lips and tossing her hair – adorably.

Even so and however adorably, being confronted by this uncomfortable truth made him drop back into silence. I was afraid he'd retreat into his shut-off self but, after stirring the fire with the poker for a bit, he stretched out again.

Ignoring the subject of his sign, he said that with some of the money Grandad would have left Mum, we'd finally be able to attend to the house.

The three of us cheered. Vee, selfish to the last, went

into a list of stuff she wanted done to her room and our bathroom – things like Californian-style closets for her clothes and a power shower like the one Farah had.

It was at this point, exactly one minute after eight o'clock, that Tiff strolled into the room through the slightly open door and jumped onto the arm of my chair.

Dad looked at her darkly and mumbled moodily but with a hint of humour, 'Ah, the Impossible Being, the cat who can talk, cook and play the piano like a virtuoso.'

'Oh no!' said Verity. 'Don't tell me Logie's given you that rubbish too about Tiff playing the piano!'

'I have, because it's true,' I said.

'Then ask her to play for us. Right now!' said Verity. 'Go on, if she can. Let's hear her.'

Tiff looked at me and shook her head, muttering quietly.

'Not now, Logan. It's not the right moment.'

'She doesn't feel like it,' I said. 'And anyway, you don't believe in her. So why should she have to prove anything to *you*?'

# Chapter 30
## GEORGE COMES HOME AND GERALD NEARLY HOLDS MY HAND

The next day, Tuesday, Dad actually phoned our school secretary and told her that due to a family bereavement I wouldn't be at school for a day or two and that Verity would be away for ten days.

Then he called the secretary of Paul's school and informed her about Paul having to go to Australia.

He himself booked the tickets to Melbourne via Singapore and Sydney – or rather got Daniel, his manager, to do it, but this had the same effect because at least he didn't leave it to his kids as he once definitely would have.

And he phoned Mum to comfort her (without us nagging him to do so) and to tell her how things were going with us.

Then it was time to fetch George because the

hospital had agreed to let him come home.

Apart from the butterfly plasters on his hands, cheeks and backside, George was his cheerful, beaming, loving self.

He insisted on having Tiff on his lap in the car (I'd insisted she come with us to fetch him). And then, when we got home, he wanted her on his bed, where we'd been told he must stay for a few days.

I hung around in his room too, reading him stories and trying to teach him to tune in to what Tiff said.

He didn't succeed but it didn't bother him. To him she was the big black cuddly cat he called Tiff Tunakins, who'd saved him from having his eyes pecked out by a deranged parrot. And that was enough. It was all he needed.

The next day I got off school again and Dad asked Greta to come over to mind George and me while he took Vee and Paul to the airport.

She brought the theatre with her in the car so that it would be 'in place' when Gerald caught the bus to our house after school.

To my delight the lights were already working at the flick of a tiny switch, which was on a small black box attached to some long leads that you could just plug into any ordinary wall socket.

Two of the six matchbox spotlights had faintly

blue-coloured mini-sized bulbs – or 'filaments' – in them. The other four were the normal colour of light.

According to Greta, Gerald had stayed up till four in the morning working on them. 'And he said to tell you he thinks he can get those filaments in both red and green, if you need them.'

Genius wizard or *what*?

When he finally arrived at about 5 pm, we used the newly electrified theatre to entertain George.

I found some old hand puppets in a box and we made up scenes and dialogue with them and sang silly songs as we went along, letting George turn the lights on and off as often as he liked.

Tiff joined in the songs which made George bounce up and down on his bed yelling, 'She's singing, she's singing, I can tell she's singing now!'

To my relief, during supper, Tiff stayed on all fours. (I don't know why, but I didn't want to have to explain about her to Greta.) And without a word of complaint, she accepted her supper in a bowl on the floor.

Greta was drinking wine – lots of it, it seemed to me – and by the time Dad got back she'd had too much to drive home.

Dad said it was no problem and that both she and Gerald should just stay the night – Greta in Vee's room and Gerald in Paul's – given that the spare room with its toxic fumes was unusable.

And later, lying snug with Tiff in my bed in the dark, it felt lovely and natural to have them staying in the house.

I said so and Tiff's reply surprised me.

'I hope it doesn't become a habit. We wouldn't want Greta taking the place of your mother, would we?'

'Of course not, and of course she won't!' I snapped. 'How could you even say such a thing. She'll have her own husband, Gerald's dad.'

But as I tried to drift off, it occurred to me how naïve I was being. There was no evidence of Gerald's dad – none. He was never mentioned. There was no reference to him.

As ever, Tiff seemed to read my thoughts.

'I think you'll find they're divorced,' she said softly. 'You should ask him.'

But in the morning – in the bustle of getting back to normal, even though it was anything but a normal morning – I forgot to ask Gerald about it, or perhaps didn't like to.

It was agreed that I'd go to school with Gerald, Greta would drive us, and Dad would look after George by himself.

We set off early so there'd be time for Gerald to go

home and change into clean school clothes. We took the theatre too so he could keep working on it (and make the front-of-stage curtains draw at the push of a button).

At their house, Greta gave us apple waffles and then Gerald and I walked down the hill to school.

As we trundled down the pot-holed hill with our heavy school bags, it was easy to bump about unevenly.

In one of the uneven bumpings, Gerald's hand knocked against mine. It was nothing, a nothing accident. But it gave me a start. Especially as – it seemed to me – he nearly used the accident to take my hand.

We fell into silence and didn't look at each other.

But we both knew that if not at that moment, then definitely sometime, we'd be walking somewhere, holding hands.

# Chapter 31
# MENTAL JAM

First thing after assembly, Miss Notts sent for me to play for Mr Crow. It was time to test out Gerald's theory of how head teachers think.

When I arrived in Miss Notts' study, Mr Crow was there. And I thought he was going to get on his knees and grovel before me.

First Miss Notts said how sorry she was to hear about my grandfather dying – though I could tell she didn't really care – being far more interested in having a child prodigy in her school.

'This is very exciting, Logan,' Mr Crow gabbled. 'Miss Notts tells me you play…like a virtuoso.'

I went (acted) all shy, hanging my head and scuffing my shoes.

'Logan,' Miss Notts beamed. 'You mustn't be

embarrassed by your talent. You must face up to it and embrace it.'

I hung and scuffed some more.

In a tiny voice I said, 'It wasn't me playing, Miss Notts. It was that feral cat.'

It didn't go down well.

'Don't be so silly, child,' she snapped. 'You're not a stupid girl, in spite of most of your grades. In fact, you are possibly very, very gifted. So why make such a ridiculous statement?'

I said nothing.

Mr Crow looked out of the window but Miss Notts did not take her eyes off me.

Eventually, her gaze softened and she said, 'At least play *something* for Mr Crow. It doesn't matter what. Anything at all.'

'Except,' I looked her straight in the eye now. 'It's the truth, Miss Notts. I can't play the piano well at all. Except for a few babyish pieces I learnt years ago and which, anyway, I've probably forgotten.'

They exchanged looks. Both of them sighed as if they wished they were in any profession but teaching.

'All right, Logan, we'll leave it for today,' said Miss Notts. 'But when you're ready, when you get over all this shyness and false modesty, I hope you'll play for us all.'

Back in the classroom, Gerald raised his eyebrows to ask how it had gone. I gave the thumbs up. Cammy saw the whole exchange and started giggling with Clarky.

After school Gerald and I walked together to the gates. Cammy and Clarky walked behind us calling out stupid things like, 'When you gonna *kiss* the ge-ne-*is*.'

Ignoring them, I related to Gerald how his theory about modesty and shyness had worked perfectly in Miss Notts' study.

He gave me a high five to celebrate and split off to walk up his hill to his white cottage, his beautiful mum and our model theatre.

The high five shut Cammy and Clarky up – though not for long.

At the bus stop, they started pushing me and giggling: *Has he snogged you yet? I bet he has. Liar, we know he has, we can tell.*

It went on the whole bus ride home.

There, to my amazement, I found George and Dad at the kitchen table playing Connect Four. Unbelievable. Dad had never played a board game with any of us in his life.

He got up and kissed me on the top of the head. He'd never done that either, as long as I could remember.

He ordered take-away pizzas for supper, finding just enough money in his wallet to pay for them – once he'd counted out and included a lot of pennies.

As Tiff didn't eat pizza I made her fishcakes – just how she liked them, with potato and parsley.

George thought the way she sat at the table and ate with us was hilarious.

He said he couldn't wait to tell his friends at school.

I suggested he didn't because they'd only accuse him of being off his trolley.

'Tiff is our family secret, George. Everyone thinks we're weird enough as it is.'

'Well, I don't know about that,' said Dad. 'I should think every family has its weird side once behind closed doors. And while we're on the subject of weirdness, Logie, you still haven't given me a good enough explanation of who Miss Notts heard playing the piano.'

'I have, Dad. It was Tiff. It's just you won't believe it.'

'It was me, indeed, Mr Dempster,' said Tiff, patting her mouth the way she did – delicately with a paper napkin. 'And I'm looking forward to playing for you.'

Dad frowned and didn't ask me what she'd said because he'd understood every word.

After supper George went back to bed and I read him a quick story before going to my room to do two important things, which were:

1) Tidy my room – organic and genius as it might be, I couldn't bear sleeping in the mess.
2) Do my homework. (I was hanging out with a genius and had a lot of every kind of work to do just to start to keep up.)

While I worked, with Tiff asleep under the table, I could faintly hear Dad playing the piano in his study. It sounded different to his usual jarring, 'non-modular' stuff.

It sounded joyful and jazzy.

By the time I'd finished my homework and Tiff and I had gone downstairs, the music had stopped, but there was a pleasant surprise awaiting us.

There was no DO NOT DISTURB sign hanging on Dad's study door. He'd taken it off when he'd invited me in (for the first time ever) and he'd *not put it back.*

'You know,' Tiff sighed, 'I think this lack of a sign *is* a sign. And we can't go on putting it off. Sooner or later, he has to hear his own music the way it's meant to sound. So let's do it.'

I knew she was right. It had to be done.

I took a deep breath and knocked.

His voice was sleepy as he called *come in*.

'Can we sit with you a bit?' I asked.

He was a little put out, I could see, but he motioned *yes*.

He waited for me to say something.

'Dad, did we hear you playing…you know…sort of jazz?'

He took a page from the music rack. 'Yes. This is…something I wrote when I was still at school.'

'You kept it all this time?'

'For some reason. It was in the safe – which I only opened after I realised someone had been in here. You, as it turned out.'

'Play it for us. Please,' I asked.

He started and it was good. In my opinion, better than anything he'd written since.

Tiff jumped onto the piano stool the better to watch his hands. When he'd finished we both asked for it again.

So he played it again, improvising a bit here and there.

When it was over the second time, Tiff said, 'There are some missing notes, Mr Dempster. May I find them?'

He didn't answer yes or no, but clearly understood and got up – leaving the piano to Tiff.

She began to play and a thrill went through me as – at last – my father was introduced to the music he *could* compose (even if he hadn't admitted it yet).

The blood drained from his face.

'Incredible,' he whispered to himself, over and over.

Then, as if unable to contain himself any longer, he picked up his trumpet from its silk-lined case...and joined in.

'Take it away, Mr Dempster!' Tiff said, turning and grinning in what I thought was a rather cheesy way.

By now, my feet were jumping. I was getting 'into the groove' too. All Dad's percussion instruments that we'd never been allowed to touch were lying around.

I picked up some shakers covered in silver balls and started working them.

The music we made was loud and, as we grew in confidence, it became louder and wilder.

So loud and wild, it brought George down in his pyjamas.

He screamed when he saw Tiff.

'*Logie!*' he yelled. '*Our cat's playing Dad's piano.*'

Like we didn't know, couldn't see it for ourselves.

'She sure is, George.' I went over and hugged him. 'Do you want to join in? You can. You can choose a percussion instrument.'

His face was red – with fear or excitement, I couldn't tell. After watching – or gawping – for a bit, he relaxed, grabbed a tom-tom and began to drum.

When the piece came to an end, Dad finished it off with a few spine-chilling blasts of his trumpet.

He flopped into his chair. 'Out of this world!' he breathed.

Then, almost at once, he jumped up.

'We should be recording this or we may not remember. Tiff, do you think we can go again?'

'Ye…ess!' George cheered.

'Actually,' said Tiff, 'if you don't mind, I'd rather play something else. I'd like to play the piece Miss Notts heard.'

Dad fiddled with his recording equipment, not looking at Tiff as he spoke.

'The piece Miss Notts heard. She said it was one of mine. So, if I'm getting this right – and believe me it isn't easy to grasp – Tiff was playing my music in the school hall?'

'I *told* you that, Dad!' I said, picking the score off the pile on the floor. 'It was this.'

210

'And yes, Mr Dempster, please do record it, for later reference,' said Tiff.

'What's she saying?' George whispered to me.

'It doesn't matter,' I whispered back. 'Just listen.'

Dad switched on his recorder and adjusted the microphone on the piano.

Tiff began to play.

Dad's mouth dropped open as his once silence-filled concerto filled the room with its soaring beauty now that its missing notes were drawn in where they belonged.

For some time, he seemed frozen – as if afraid any tiny movement might shatter the moment.

Then he snatched up a pencil and scribbled away on his score.

When the music came to an end, George and I clapped and said, 'Bravo,' very quietly.

'My god,' said Dad. 'Now I see what Miss Notts meant when she said it was "truly beautiful". I do, I do.'

As if what she'd just done was completely ordinary, Tiff jumped off the piano stool and went towards Dad's trumpet.

'I wonder,' she asked politely. 'Do you think you could play piano while I have a go on this?'

Dad shook himself, as if forcing himself out of his shock and disbelief.

He took his newly scribbled-on score, set it on the rack and played Tiff's version of his concerto.

And though she didn't really have the breath for it, Tiff did her best to introduce the trumpet.

This, in turn, got George going with a pair of maracas from the glass cabinet. He danced round rattling them – a bundle of joy in his baggy pyjamas and butterfly plasters.

I sat in Dad's armchair, drinking in the unimaginable sight.

When the piece was over, Dad played some of it back on the recorder to check he'd got it.

Then he closed the piano, put the trumpet back in its case and rubbed his eyes.

'Well, this is going to take some getting my head round. Meanwhile, what have we done here? What music have we made?'

George gave the maracas a triumphant shake and said, 'Our own mental music, Dad. Much better than yours.'

# Chapter 32
## CARTHAGE COMES TO LIFE AND A NEW SIGN

Daniel, Dad's manager, went completely crazy when he heard Dad's new piece, now titled *Concerto for a Cat and Trumpet*.

And by Saturday he'd just about moved in. He was on his mobile every minute, pacing round, eating non-stop on the hoof and talking. He must have spoken to everyone who was anyone in the world of experimental music and even non-experimental music – setting up meetings, a recording, someone to work with Dad on the orchestration, musicians for a recording, a premiere, musicians for the premiere.

He was excited beyond belief about 'his client's new work' and he was transmitting his excitement to anyone who would listen.

'I knew it!' he yelled, raiding our fridge (Greta must

have been stocking it as it was always full). 'Your father is a genius and at last he's drawing it down. I had the faith. No one can say I didn't.'

Once, I started to say, 'Well, actually, Daniel, it wasn't Dad who drew it down it was…'

But Tiff interrupted. 'Don't, Logie…don't even go there.'

Daniel stared. 'If I didn't know better, I'd say that cat just spoke.' He laughed a searing laugh, grabbed his ringing phone and dashed outside to pace the long grass and converse excitedly.

He wasn't the only one who was excited.

I was over the moon. As it was Saturday, Greta brought Gerald over with our theatre. It now had more lights than we'd ever need (George had added another two rows), even for the most ambitious production of *Carthage* – as we'd decided our show would be called. (It would tell the story of a love affair between a Carthaginian general's daughter and a mercenary, but only as an excuse for a series of fantastic battles.)

Greta had already designed some sets for it. She laid out some drawings on the kitchen table.

Gerald and I winked at each other as we had no intention of touching them. This was our show and we were going to create every bit of it ourselves.

214

Her designs set Daniel on fire though: *Perhaps Dad and Greta could work together? Perhaps Greta could design the sets and costumes for one of Dad's old operas, which would be rewritten in his new Cat and Trumpet style?* There was no end to Daniel's ambitions for my father now.

Leaving them to their excitements, Gerald and I took our theatre into the sitting room.

Gerald had brought books on the Carthaginian wars with illustrations. I got to work, tracing them.

'You're good at this,' said Gerald, watching me transfer a tracing of a shield onto card. 'Our designs are going to be much better than Mum's. We mustn't let her interfere.'

'I agree,' I said. 'And I've just had an idea. For one of the battle scenes we could have rows and rows of these shields attached together and then we can move the whole lot at the same time to look like an advancing army.'

'Fantastic,' said Gerald. 'Let me help.'

I glowed like hot coal.

We worked for hours – tracing armour, tents, horses, elephants, Carthaginian warriors and their mercenaries (paid soldiers) from every corner of the then known world – though in this case mostly North Africa.

As we traced, transferred and painted, we talked about how we'd make our characters and effects work. And realised we'd need more materials. More glue. Plywood to back the card characters. Dowel rods, mini-motors. Gloves to hide our hands when we moved the characters. A jigsaw.

'Maybe your dad has one?' said Gerald, which made me laugh at the idea of Dad owning a single tool.

'I wish we could go to town now and get what we need,' I said.

'We can,' said Gerald and we did. That's how things worked with him. You wanted something. You needed something. You went and got it.

He just went straight up to Greta and asked if she'd take us.

She said she would because she had some shopping to do anyway.

She dropped us off outside Ragden's art and craft shop, saying she'd collect us there in an hour and a half.

Gerald reminded her that shopping requires money. Without a single moan or groan (like my mother always gave) she whipped out two twenty-pound notes – hooted – and drove away.

At the art shop we got more sheets of thick white

card, clear acrylic glue, small pots of paint and a pack of plastic gloves I planned to somehow dye so our hands would blend into the background when we moved our characters.

We went to a timber yard hidden down a lane where Gerald was greeted by the man behind the counter like an old friend. He gave us all the wood off-cuts Gerald chose for absolutely nothing.

Then he *lent* us one of his own jigsaws – just like that – when Gerald explained that his was back at his house and we hadn't enough money to buy a second one.

We went to an electrical shop where Gerald searched out some miniature motors with which he planned to motorise the arms and maybe even the legs of our plywood-backed main characters.

By now we'd spent more than forty pounds but Gerald wasn't bothered. He produced other money – his pocket money, I supposed – and I loved his attitude, which was: *If we need it for* Carthage, *we get it.* How far away was that from what went on in our house? A million miles.

He suggested we go for a milkshake, and led the way to a coffee bar in yet another lane I didn't know existed.

Here a waitress greeted him by name.

'How come everyone knows you?' I asked as we slurped our shakes.

'My dad lives here in Ragden,' he said awkwardly, looking anywhere but at me. 'I come here a lot.'

I blushed for him, but I had to get this out in the open while I had the chance.

'So…are your parents…?'

'Yes, they are.'

The word 'divorced' was not spoken. It was too dreaded to pronounce.

In the car on the way home, Greta said, 'Logan, your father's asked us to stay for supper. I bought some lovely fresh fish at the market. I hope you like fish?'

I didn't like it much so I said, 'Well, Tiff does. Hope you got enough for her to have a big helping!'

It made Greta laugh.

The supper turned out to be fishy and dangerous.

George nearly let 'the cat out of the bag' gabbling on to Greta and Daniel about how they should see Tiff play the piano and the trumpet.

Greta and Daniel played along, humouring him.

George sensed that that was what they were doing and got cross. 'No, tell them, Dad, she *really* does play the piano and trumpet.'

Dad muttered. And I could see he didn't want it

out – that his new concerto was as much, if not more, Tiff's work than his.

Gerald stepped in, bold as brass.

'I think it's a family secret, George, best not go on about it.'

'Why?' said George.

'Because if it gets out what Tiff can do, she'll become a freak show.'

'What, on television?' said George.

Dad started a 'grown-up' conversation with Greta and Daniel, distracting them, dismissing our talk as kids' talk.

'Yes, on TV,' Gerald said to George.

'Well, I'd love that. It would be cool because we'd have to go on too, with her, as her owners. And then we'd soon be rich and I could have a PlayStation like everyone else in our class.'

'You're going to get a PlayStation anyway, George. When Dad's new concerto is a great success,' I said. 'I promise you will – but only if you stop going on about Tiff. In fact *only* if you promise not to tell *anyone* what you saw in Dad's study?'

Later that night, when Daniel had driven away, Greta and Gerald had gone to bed in Verity and Paul's rooms and Tiff had gone for a late-night walk, George came knocking at my door.

'What'll we tell Mum about Tiff when she gets back?'

Tears trickled down his face. Not surprisingly. He was missing her so much and he'd been so brave.

'Oh, Georgie Porgie.' I made a place for him beside me on the bed and stroked his butterfly plasters. 'Mum's in the family. Of course, you – we – can tell her about Tiff. Just not people outside.'

He begged to be allowed to sleep in my bed.

I said OK. We'd go top to bottom if he promised not to kick my face.

We arranged ourselves and he said softly, 'Seems like Greta and Gerald are moving in. Will Mum be home soon?'

'Next Saturday,' I said. 'Six days to go. Not long.'

For me the six days went like the wind, as each afternoon after school I either went to Gerald's to work on *Carthage* or Greta brought Gerald and the theatre round to ours and we worked there.

Our house was alive as I'd never known it – there was laughter and music – with doors open everywhere, including Dad's study – and much excitement as plans for the premiere of *Concerto for a Cat and Trumpet* came together.

Daniel and the musicians were in and out talking and playing. And Greta – all the time Greta – wafted about, flashing her smile, smelling of oil paint and expensive scent, vibrant as Dad's new music – and as beautiful to behold.

By Friday evening we'd all worked together – Greta directing – to get everything as welcoming as we could for Mum.

There were fresh flowers everywhere. A fridge full of food. Laundry baskets empty. Ironing done (Greta did that). Clean sheets on the beds, coats hung up, boots in the boot cupboard, skateboards in a neat row. Even the grass had been cut. Greta easily persuaded Dad to do it. How? Mum never had, not once.

The house couldn't have looked or felt less like the house Mum had left.

It was after we'd seen Greta and Gerald off into the night and Tiff and I were going upstairs to bed, that I saw the new sign, hanging on the hook on Dad's study door. Was it a joke? Greta's idea and Greta's doing? Or was it Dad himself?

Whatever it was, the sign now hanging there said: DO DISTURB.

# Chapter 33
# I DO DISTURB AND DAD RISES TO THE OCCASION

So it had to happen and it was going to sooner or later. But now? This night? I might have been Verity, crying *why why why*?

On the way to bed I went to the loo and there it was – staring up at me. The red mark – the blood – that meant, according to Cammy, *I was now a woman.*

*Well, I'm not ready to be one*, I screamed silently.

I put some loo paper in my pants and, close to tears, went to my room. Tiff was on the bed, sitting up, her yellow eyes wide. She knew. Of course, she knew.

I buried my face in a pillow.

Now it had begun there could be no going back. There would be periods for ever. One to be dealt with every month, slowing me down, holding me up, making everything else come to a stop while I got through it, robbing my life of normal time to be getting on brilliantly with Gerald and building theatres and making up shows and loving being the Logan I'd only recently had a chance to become.

Tiff fetched tissues for my tears and put her paws round me.

When I'd cried and blown enough we got practical.

I knew there were no sanitary towels in the house because of Vee's crisis with *her* period.

I had to somehow get through the night and then get up at 5 am and go all the way to the airport to fetch Mum, Vee and Paul. Tissues in knickers would never be enough for all that.

'There's nothing for it,' said Tiff. 'You must ask your father to take you to the all-night shop.'

'I can't go in and buy sanitary towels. No way!' I cried. 'I'd die of shame. Everyone would *know*.'

'Then he must go and get them for you.'

'He never would. He'd be so embarrassed. And I'm embarrassed to even tell him,' I said. 'Oh, if only Mum was here or Vee – or Greta or even Mrs Everett.'

'Nonsense!' Tiff jumped off the bed and went to the door. 'This is no reflection on you. You haven't done something *wrong*. Hormones do what they do. They have their own life. All you have to do is manage them. So what's to be embarrassed about? Now, come on. We're going downstairs.'

She sniffed under the door. 'He's still in his study and the sign on his door says DO DISTURB. So disturb him. Go in and ask for what you need. And if he's embarrassed, that's his problem not yours. But my feeling is he'll rise to the occasion. He's changing by the hour, Logie. Opening up like a garden in spring. Now, here we go. Are you ready?'

We went downstairs. I knocked. He opened the door.

'Logie! Not in bed?' He noticed my red eyes. 'What is it?'

I looked down at Tiff looking up at me. She did her double-eyed blink.

I surprised myself by being quite cool.

'It's my period. I've got it. So can you go to the all-night garage and get me...?'

He did a Tiff-style double blink and then went into action like I was about to have a baby or something right there in the hall.

'Of course, of course. Where are my keys?'

He rushed about, found his keys, ran out of the back door and was back in moments.

'Money...' he patted all his pockets. 'I haven't got

225

any... I gave what Daniel brought me to Greta...for the shopping.'

He dashed to his study – we followed – and he started searching the mantelpiece, the CD table and then down the sides of his armchair, all the time muttering, 'My wallet, my wallet.'

Tiff went out of the room and came back with it.

'In the kitchen,' she said, 'under your sweater.'

The wallet was empty of money too – except for two twenty-pence pieces – but there was a card.

'What about this?' I said. 'You can use the card.'

But the card had expired and Mum, apparently, had taken the replacement and only other card they had between them to Australia.

'Then a cheque?' I cried, hardly able to believe I had a father who could be so unworldly, so without *material means*.

'Your mother or Daniel writes the cheques...' he said – at least looking as sheepish as he should have looked.

Tiff padded over to the trumpet – glinting in its silk lining.

'Take this and leave it as security on going back to pay in the morning,' she said.

'My trumpet?' Dad sounded appalled. Then, darting a look at me and my tear-stained face he said, 'Well, I suppose it's only a trumpet, after all.'

He snapped the case closed and dashed away with it.

And must have driven there and back like the wind because he didn't seem to be gone that long.

We heard him screech up the driveway and, still rushing and flustered, he ran back into the kitchen.

I didn't know whether to laugh or cry.

He had bought...everything, just everything. He must have taken one packet or box of every product for periods that the all-night garage store had on its shelves!

# Chapter 34
## MUM COMES HOME AND TIFF LEAVES

As promised, Mum, Paul and Vee came through the airport doors at 7 am the next morning.

I noticed immediately. There was something different about Mum. She was sunburned and smoothed. No tired lines. Even though her father had just died, her eyes weren't sad.

Dad folded her up in his arms and she let him and he stood there holding her, his head buried in her hair.

I'd never seen that before.

And in a way nothing was the same in our house again.

Grandad had left Mum and her brother his house in Melbourne, his car and his money, which turned out to be quite a lot. Because her brother was taking the house and car, we got most of the money.

First up was a new boiler and radiators, and to my relief our house was freed of toxic fumes.

A firm of serious builders came next and some badly needed underpinning was done to the house's foundations.

There were no Californian closets and no power shower for Vee because Mum said it was more important to keep some of the money for our 'future education'.

There was a new cooker though. A great orange Aga like Greta's.

And there was lots of redecorating.

'But not so as to lose the character of this wonderful house,' said Greta, who was becoming closer friends with Mum by the day.

This was brilliant for me as it meant Gerald and I could easily keep going and finish *Carthage*.

When we felt it was as ready as it would ever be, we performed it in our model theatre in front of the whole school – Gerald doing all the men's voices and me doing the two female voices (the general's daughter and the moon – oh yes, we had a talking moon because the Carthaginians worshipped the moon). And, amazingly, my throat didn't close and I could breathe while I performed – though probably because I was behind the theatre and couldn't actually be seen!

Dad, Mum, Daniel and Greta were special guests at the back, sitting with Miss Notts. (By the way, Dad had come up trumps and saved my bacon with regard to me being a child prodigy pianist to make Ofsted sit up and listen. He'd phoned Miss Notts and told her that the virtuoso playing in the hall certainly wasn't his daughter. He said that the children must have had some kind of recording they were playing. And would she let the whole matter drop – just this once? She did and so did Mr Crow.)

But back to our performance of *Carthage*: admittedly, no one, not even Gerald and I, fully understood the story but thanks to Gerald's electronic wizardry and my brilliant designs – no one noticed or cared, and it was a complete smash hit.

I was no longer plain, pug-nosed Logan with no friends.

I was the starry theatre-maker who was in with Gerald and who *everyone* wanted to be seen with.

Daniel was so impressed by our show he wanted Dad – who we'd allowed to write some battle-scene music – to develop it into a full-scale opera.

Thankfully they soon dropped the idea. *Carthage* was what had brought Gerald and me together.

It was ours and we didn't want anyone touching it or 'developing' it.

And all the time Mum and Greta's friendship was getting stronger. Which was surprising, as anyone – even Mum, you would have thought – could see that Dad was in love with Greta. As soon as she came into the house, he'd come bounding out of the study, his face lit up like a torch.

But, I'm glad to say, he was also in love with Mum all over again. I'd never seen them the way they were now, eyes following each other, sitting close, listening to each other intently.

Once, on the afternoon of Dad's premiere of *Cat and Trumpet* (which was how we all referred to the Tiff/Dad concerto) I caught them kissing against a kitchen counter.

It was a case of feeling a bit *yuck*. You want your parents to love each other but you never want to witness the 'in love' part that closely.

Although, if I'd had to choose between the way they'd been before Mum went to Australia, and catching them kissing in the kitchen, I'd have taken the kissing any day of the week.

As for the premiere of *Cat and Trumpet*, well, talk about dreams coming true. It was almost exactly the way I'd imagined it in Dad's armchair, the night

Tiff first drew down the missing notes.

We were all there in our own box...Mum, Vee, Paul, George, Greta, Gerald, Daniel and, on my insistence, Tiff.

As in my imagination, Mum was glowing and bejewelled (in her mother's jewels, which her father had given her before he died). Dad was tall and handsome, conducting in white tie. And when it was all over, the audience *did* give a standing ovation, yelling many 'bravos'.

And even if it didn't exactly rain down with first-night flowers, two big bouquets were brought onto the stage – one for Dad and one for the first violinist.

Of course, I'd suggested that Dad should call Tiff up to take a bow along with him and the orchestra. But in the interests of not being the weirdest family in the world, I had not pushed for it.

And nor did Tiff. She wasn't pushing for anything.

Since Mum had returned Tiff was becoming more and more of a normal cat with every hour that passed.

In fact, from the day we picked Mum up at the airport, I don't think I ever saw her stand up and walk on her back legs. She never asked to sit at table and eat with us or suggested she show Mum how well she could cook. And certainly she never touched the piano or trumpet in our house again.

She still slept on my bed and purred like a motorbike when I stroked her and she still did her double-eyed yellow wink when there was something secret for us to share.

But we stopped talking the way we had before, and when one wintry morning I woke to see her sitting at the dressing table with the lamp on, staring out of the misted-up window, I knew she was going to leave.

I took her in my arms, buried my face in her fur and let myself cry. 'You came to me when I needed you, Tiff, and you've changed everything. Thank you. But I know what's going to happen now and I know it has to. I know you've got other things to do and other people to go to.'

She purred and blinked, licked at my tears and butted her head against my chin.

'I'll come down to the kitchen and see you out,' I said. 'But first…'

I took the coral necklace she'd tried on the first morning in my room and put it round her neck. 'To remember me by.'

And I'm sure I heard through her purring. 'Thanks. It always did suit me well.'

# Chapter 35
## BACK TO NOW, MEMORIES FAIL AND MY FAMILY SAYS I'M MAD

I'm writing this eight years after that morning when Tiff walked out of our back door.

I've done some counting and realise that, besides me, there were six people who witnessed all, or at least some, of the amazing things Tiff did for me and our family.

They were:

> My father
> Paul
> Verity
> George
> Mrs Everett
> Gerald

Today, apart from me, there is only one person on that

list who acknowledges it or even remembers that she talked, cooked and played the piano (brilliantly) and the trumpet (not very well).

The other five agree that I found a cat in the garden soon after Mum left for Australia. They agree I brought her inside and that the next day she went to the Burton Animal Rescue Home.

They admit that a black cat – which we did keep for a while – appeared as if from nowhere and saved George from having his eyes pecked out by Mrs Everett's sick parrot.

But that is it. They claim they can't even be sure that the cat who saved George was the same cat we took to the Rescue Home. *Why would it be?* they all say. *If it was in the Rescue Home, how could it have been in our garden at that moment when George was being attacked?*

If I remind them I'd run off to Burton and helped her escape and that's how she'd been there, they say...*whatever.*

If I remind Vee and Paul how Tiff helped cook up the festive spaghetti that first evening after George had gone to hospital, Paul laughs, 'Logie, you always had an insane imagination.'

And Vee does her screwy finger at the forehead thing to say: *You're crackers.*

And when I beg Dad and George to remember the night of the 'mental music jam' in his study, they say there was a cat there all right, on the arm of the chair, but they both deny she touched, let alone played, the piano or trumpet.

'You should definitely see a shrink!' George cries, now a spotty teenager who knows everything (I still adore him though). 'How could a cat play the piano? Cats don't have fingers and where would a cat get the breath to play the trumpet?'

Of course, what he says makes sense. But he is wrong.

If I accost Dad about how he arrived at the version of *Concerto for a Cat and Trumpet* that he's now well-known for, with all its untypical (for him) modular beauty, he has his story off pat. 'I found a piece I'd kept in my safe since music school. I was inspired. I developed it into *Cat and Trumpet*. It was one of those things. It just happened to work!'

(Strange then, I long to say but don't out of politeness, that you've never written anything so beautiful since, even if your music does now have more notes in it than silence.)

Even Gerald, who I'd so loved in those days (though not any more, he's just too scientific), has a theory to explain Tiff as a figment of my imagination.

'The cat arrived in your life at the exact moment of your greatest need,' he lectured when we last met for a coffee in Ragden. 'Your mother had abandoned you – or that's how you felt. A stranger had moved in who you'd taken an instant dislike to. Your father didn't communicate and shut himself away all the time. So to get you through all this, your psyche kicked in and projected your needs onto a cat you found in the garden. She didn't really talk, cook or play the piano. She just did in your mind – out of your need for *something* to get you through. It's called "transference" by psychologists. Or sometimes "externalisation".'

'But,' I yelped at him, making everyone in the coffee shop turn and stare, 'you understood her yourself. And you heard her play in the school hall. That day Miss Notts came in. And if Tiff wasn't playing, who was?'

'You were, of course! I saw you with my own eyes,' he said calmly. 'It was amazing. Like you were possessed by some sudden flash of musical genius. These things happen and can be explained by neurologists. It's like when a parent sees their child trapped under a car and suddenly finds the strength to lift the car. But whoever was playing, it certainly wasn't a cat! That would have been impossible!'

I asked him if *he* was losing his mind and his memory – and all so young – paid the bill and left the coffee shop.

And how glad I am now that I never did anything more than hold hands with Gerald on a few occasions after *Carthage* had been a smash hit. Gerald the Genius who had, and still has to have, a scientific explanation for everything even when there isn't one. The boy who can so easily call impossible what he saw and heard with his own eyes and ears. It amazed me. How could anyone forget or deny the effect Tiff had?

# Chapter 36
# THE TIFF EFFECT

And that evening, after that coffee with Gerald, I sat down and made a kind of chart.

I headed it THE TIFF EFFECT – although, I suppose, it could also have been headed THE CRACKED PAVING-STONE EFFECT, because as I said at the beginning of all this, if my grandfather hadn't tripped over that paving stone on a Melbourne pavement, none of what happened to me and our family would have happened.

I tried to keep the chain of events that changed my life as simple as I could in The Chart. It wasn't easy as there were so many tangents I could have gone off on.

But this is what I arrived at:

∞ Because a paving stone was cracked, my grandfather tripped and broke his hip.

∞ Because his hip broke, my mother went away.

∞ Because my mother went away, Mrs Everett and her child-hating parrot moved in and Vee fled to Farah's.

∞ Because of the above I felt abandoned and decided to become impossible.

∞ Because I was being impossible I met Tiff.

∞ Because I met Tiff, George was saved from Mrs E's parrot's attack.

∞ Because Tiff saved George (and Mrs E left) I was allowed to keep her.

∞ Because I kept her she encouraged me to disturb Dad and took me into Dad's study.

∞ Because we disturbed Dad and went into his study, Tiff gave him *Concerto for a Cat and Trumpet*.

∞ And because Tiff gave him *Concerto for a Cat and Trumpet* (plus a few other things, like the influence of Greta, because without Tiff I wouldn't have got in with Gerald, and Greta wouldn't have come to our house), Dad vacated the Slot he'd been hogging. He stopped being the mad loner, shut off from everyone, writing music with more silences in

242

it than notes that only forty-seven people in the world were interested in.

AND THIS IS THE POINT THAT SHOWS THE TRUE TIFF EFFECT:
∞ Because Dad vacated that Slot, it became free, empty, mine to take if I wanted it. *And I did want it.* Without realising it, *I'd always wanted it.*

And in that Slot I have become what I was always meant to be: a loner, or, as I prefer to call it, '*happy in my own company*', at theatre design school, designing sets and costumes so *experimental*, probably only forty-nine people in the world would understand them. And here's the thing: *I love it!*

# Chapter 37

## LAST WORD, OR WHAT THE BOY GENIUS CAN'T EXPLAIN

Anyway, why do I argue with Gerald or anyone else about Tiff? I'm disappointed Gerald can't suspend his belief that if something can't be explained scientifically it doesn't exist, but I don't need his say-so, or anyone else's, to make what I know to be true, true.

You see, the one person on the list of people who heard Tiff talk and who now doesn't deny it, is Mrs Everett.

We became real friends after Mum came back from Australia. And if Tiff's extraordinariness was a figment of my imagination, an 'externalisation' or 'transference' of my need, then it would be good if Gerald the Genius/Great Scientist or anyone else could explain the following:

How come when I visit Mrs E, Tiff is there too – sipping tea and talking with us so we perfectly understand?

How come that on some of these occasions, if you walk past the house, you'll hear the piano part of Howard Dempster's famous *Concerto for a Cat and Trumpet*?

And how come, if you peered through the window, you wouldn't see me or Mrs Everett at the piano but Tiff – wearing a coral necklace – and playing like the *possible being* she actually is?

# More Red Apples you might enjoy . . .

£4.99

978 1 84616 327 2

Hi, it's Maddy Blue here and I'm a total mag-hag – addicted to magazines! When I'm feeling mad, sad or bad, I buy myself one, crawl between the bright, shiny pages and get lost for ever. (*Some people wish I would…*) So can they help when I fail an Envy Exam and fall out with my best friends? Blusherama!!!

If my life was a magazine, would it be a glitzy, glossy number or a downmarket cheapie? You be the judge…

£5.99

978 1 84362 549 0

Lulu Baker's dad has a new love,
Varaminta le Bone. She's a sizzling
sensation…and pure poison. How can Lulu
make her dad see Varaminta for who she really is?
A mysterious recipe book and some *very*
unusual ingredients just might do the trick…

978 1 84362 689 3    £5.99

As Lulu scales new heights with her enchanted
recipe book, she discovers that the evil
Varaminta is looming again – and this time
she has joined forces with an international
arch villain! Lulu faces her greatest challenges
yet... Will she be rendered powerless or can she
overcome them to gain a happy ending?

978 1 84616 215 2    £4.99

Chloe Wells doesn't have many friends – none,
to be precise. But she's quite happy with her
life, until she ends up in hospital with
a shattered femur and discovers how much she
has been missing out on. Away from her rather
unusual family, Chloe begins to question
exactly why she's always been protected from
the world and raised to be perfect – just like
a hothouse flower.

978 1 84362 560 5    £4.99

Jelly Jackson may not be good at anything
else, but she's a star when it comes to shooting
goals! So when her beloved game is taken
away from her, Jelly's determined to fight –
even if it means shooting her mouth off too!
Jelly's about to prove that there's more than
one way to be a star.

GILL LOBEL

When her mum is taken into hospital, Pearl goes to live with a foster family. But all Pearl really wants is to be back with her mum on their narrow boat. And when her mum runs away from the hospital, Pearl knows she must go back to the boat to find her…

978 1 84121 435 1    £4.99

Warning! Snoopers watch out! Fierce
guard-bunny on patrol! So paws off this
book! That includes my friend, Cassie. And
especially Mum. Who's FAR too busy
drooling over creepy-crawly Action Man
to care what I think anyway.

# More Orchard Red Apples

| | | |
|---|---|---|
| Clarice Bean, Don't Look Now | Lauren Child | 978 1 84616 507 8 |
| Clarice Bean Spells Trouble | Lauren Child | 978 1 84362 858 3★ |
| Utterly Me, Clarice Bean | Lauren Child | 978 1 84362 304 5★ |
| Cupid Cakes | Fiona Dunbar | 978 1 84362 688 6 |
| Pink Chameleon | Fiona Dunbar | 978 1 84616 230 5★ |
| River Song | Belinda Hollyer | 978 1 84362 943 6★ |
| The Truth About Josie Green | Belinda Hollyer | 978 1 84362 885 9 |
| My Scary Fairy Godmother | Rose Impey | 978 1 84362 683 1 |
| Do Not Read Any Further | Pat Moon | 978 1 84121 456 6 |
| Do Not Read Or Else | Pat Moon | 978 1 84616 082 0 |

All priced at £4.99, except for those marked ★ which are £5.99. *Clarice Bean, Don't Look Now* is £6.99.

Orchard Red Apples are available from all good bookshops, or can be ordered direct from the publisher: Orchard Books, PO BOX 29, Douglas IM99 1BQ
Credit card orders please telephone 01624 836000
or fax 01624 837033 or visit our website: www.wattspub.co.uk
or e-mail: bookshop@enterprise.net for details.

To order please quote title, author and ISBN
and your full name and address.
Cheques and postal orders should be made payable to 'Bookpost plc.'
Postage and packing is FREE within the UK
(overseas customers should add £1.00 per book).

Prices and availability are subject to change.